PARANORMAL DOUBLE PACK

PICTURE PERFECT
&
REBORN

JAYNE RYLON

PARANORMAL DOUBLE PACK

Contains Picture Perfect & Reborn by Jayne Rylon
Published by Happy Endings Publishing
Copyright 2007 Jayne Rylon
Edited by Raelene Gorlinsky & Mary Moran
Cover Art by Angela Waters
Formatted by IRONHORSE Formatting

contact@JayneRylon.com

www.JayneRylon.com

Sign Up for the Naughty News. Twenty-five subscribers **win prizes** in
each edition! http://www.JayneRylon.com/newsletter

Facebook.com/jaynerylon

@JayneRylon on Twitter

Get personalized autographed books, t-shirts, hoodies, totes and more
at www.JayneRylon.com/shop

ISBN-13: 978-1-94178-508-9

CONTENTS

PICTURE PERFECT
JAYNE RYLON

PROLOGUE
Ireland, Twelfth century

"Do you love me?"

Conn peered down into the adoring eyes of the alluring young witch. Lying beside him on the forest floor, the light dappled her fair skin. Her chest rose and fell rapidly as she recovered from their frolicking dash through the trees. Enchantment surrounded her, lounging on a bed of leaves, raven hair strewn about her delicate frame. A word away from her surrender, he refused to lie to her.

"Deirdre, I care for you."

"But you don't love me." Though her eyes flashed with hurt, her tone reflected resignation. He honored their pact to settle for nothing less, despite the consequences.

"I'm sorry." The words were soft but final. Conn let the regret and longing that ached inside him flow through his kiss.

It was goodbye.

Deirdre relaxed beneath him as though absorbing each scrap of emotion from the final contact. He retrieved his sword from the mossy ground, buckled it over his tunic and then swung a leg over the stallion waiting at the side of the clearing. "I never meant to hurt you."

Rising in front of him, she blocked his path. The flowing silver gown draped around her. Its embroidered belt, which proclaimed her high rank, cinched her waist, emphasizing her figure as she spread her arms wide. Power crackled through the air as tears dripped from her midnight eyes and dropped silently to the forest floor.

"Conn." The plea in her voice could not be mistaken. "I'm sorry also. Someday you'll understand that true love means doing what's right even at great personal cost."

A sudden, unnatural heat enveloped Conn, starting with his legs and spreading up his torso. Panic accompanied it, causing him to struggle with a desperation reserved for survival. "Deirdre! What are you doing? Stop this!"

"Remember that I loved you."

CHAPTER ONE
October 30th, Present day

A shrill ring burst from Dana Kavanagh's pocket as she wrestled the bags of groceries onto the kitchen counter. After consulting the display of her cell, she rolled her eyes then flipped it open.

"Yes, Jenny, I still plan on going out with you tonight."

"Dana, I'm so sorry but it looks like I'm going to have to work late."

"Awesome!" Dana did a dorky happy dance as she eyed the carton of melting ice cream and the new book she'd just set down.

Jenny's chuckle carried over the phone line. "Not so fast, you don't get off the hook that easily."

"It's my birthday. Can't I spend it however I want?" Dana groaned.

"No!" Jenny's exasperation transferred over the phone. "A girl only turns thirty once, you have to do it with style."

"Does 'with style' really mean 'in a club, consuming a lot of alcohol'?" Somewhere loud and trendy would be par for the course with Jenny. Not that Dana disliked a night out on the town every now and then, but she didn't feel the need to visit each bar in the city the way her best friend seemed to.

"And hot guys. Don't forget the hot guys."

"I hate to break it to you, Jenny, but I don't know very many unattached hot guys."

"Exactly why you need to get out more!"

Dana sighed. "Listen, I really do appreciate the thought. But lately I feel like hanging out at home. It's not a national emergency, I'm just tired of meeting the same kind of man. I need a break. A change." The metrosexual guys who worried about the caloric content of their fancy-named drinks and loved drama more than a housewife addicted to soap operas got old quick for Dana.

"Then I think you're going to like my idea even more. I want you to come with me tomorrow night instead. There's a private costume party for All Hallow's Eve at my brother's estate. It will be exclusive, sophisticated and more reserved than any club."

"I don't know, Jenny. I always feel out of place there." Wealth and prestige seeped from the sprawling mansion and sculpted grounds. Even the sincere welcome of Jenny's family couldn't eclipse Dana's unease. She might knock over a priceless vase or use the wrong fork at dinner. "Besides, I don't have a costume."

"I knew you were going to say that." Jenny sounded smug. "And I know just what you should wear. The dress."

"My grandmother's dress?"

"Yes! You'll look stunning. You can be a princess."

Dana had to admit the idea held some appeal. The dress called to her. It looked like something straight out of a fairy tale. And when else could she wear it? *What the hell, why not?*

"Okay. I'll do it, but you have to help me with my hair."

"Deal! I've got to get back to work. I'll be over around five tomorrow. Happy birthday!"

* * * * *

Dana let the water run while putting away the groceries. Afterward, she gathered her romantic comedy, dessert and a glass of inexpensive riesling. The corner Jacuzzi, now filled with fragrant foam, beckoned from the bathroom. Setting her things on the tiled ledge surrounding the whirlpool, she stripped before sinking into the steamy water. One of the few luxuries in her utilitarian condo, the tub invoked a rare serenity while she indulged in a lengthy bubble bath surrounded by dozens of flickering votive candles. The diffused light, the swish of the water around her, and the creamy taste of the fudge twist ice cream soothed nerves frayed by her hectic schedule. Dana reveled in the relaxed atmosphere of the evening. *Who says this isn't the best way to spend a birthday?* Somehow it felt as if she was trying to convince herself, to cover the longing for someone to share the night with.

Embracing the opportunity to pamper herself, she went all-out. She shaved her legs, gave herself a manicure and even painted her toenails. Next, she pulled a jar of wax from her cabinet, intending to shape her eyebrows.

What the hell?

She put enough on the heating plate to do a bikini job while she was at it. Making good use of all the feminine lotions and potions lined up neatly on her sink, she dabbed, swabbed, exfoliated, slathered and buffed herself to perfection.

Or as close as she could get, anyway.

Eventually, the cloud of steam filling the bathroom dissipated, granting her a glimpse of her reflection in the mirror. She hunted for signs of aging but didn't discover much to complain about. A few laugh lines fringed her eyes and a couple extra pounds, which got harder to fight off each year, clung to her hips. But cataloging the minor deteriorations didn't bother her much.

Wet and unstyled, her strawberry blonde curls hung darker and longer—nearly to her waist—but in all the tangles, she didn't spy a single gray hair. She appraised her face as unexceptional but people frequently complimented the shade of her eyes, amusing her with words such as luminous and emerald when they were simply green. Satisfied, she pulled on a satin nightdress then headed out to enjoy her book. She sighed, squashing the disappointment tensing her shoulders at the sight of her empty bed.

A cool breeze raised goose bumps on her arms and tightened her nipples as she made her way across the room.

That's weird, where's that coming from?

Glancing at the window, she verified it remained closed against the crisp autumn air. A movement in her peripheral

7

vision caught her eye but she dismissed it. The painting on the wall opposite her bed often played tricks with the light and her perception. Maybe it teased her other senses now too. She swore the change in temperature had something to do with the canvas hanging over her dresser.

"Good evening." Dana curtsied briefly before climbing into bed. She conversed with the man in the painting on a regular basis, though she would never admit it. Her fascination with him had begun as a child and only grown since. "How are you tonight? Doing well? Yes, me too. It's my birthday, you know. I guess most people would think thirty years old is probably too old to keep talking to a silly painting like you're some imaginary friend, but I can't seem to help myself."

Down pillows engulfed her slim figure as she reclined against the headboard to study the artwork. The heirloom portrait had been in her grandmother's family for as long as anyone could recall. Vivid colors swirled across the canvas, creating a captivating image. The flickers her young imagination had mistaken for motion were nothing more than optical illusions, but that cognizance didn't lessen her infatuation. She tended to use the painting as some women used diaries. Working out her troubles or recounting the highlights of her day helped her to organize her thoughts and provided an emotional release.

"Jenny had to cancel tonight. That's okay, I guess. I didn't really feel like putting on an act anyway. What am I going to do, Conn? I'm so tired of being alone, but I can't seem to find the right man. It takes so much energy to put myself out there when I already think it's hopeless." Dana continued rambling, speaking her thoughts as they occurred, without any filters to alter her innermost fears. Not even with Jenny could she say the same.

"Did you ever find *the one*? Was she the artist who painted you? I want someone who sees me. Really sees me, like I see the man inside you when I look at this portrait." Something about the handsome man sitting proudly astride his gray horse compelled her. His eyes drew her attention every time she so much as glanced in his direction. Intensity radiated from their depths.

She wondered, not for the first time, who he had been. The fancy banner waving below his feet proclaimed him *Sir Conn*

Hennessy but his elaborate clothing and regal bearing told her more about the subject who'd inspired such glorious imagery. Surely, no artist could have imagined a man like this. No, he'd been real. She knew it just as certainly as she knew anger burned in his eyes.

Forever frozen, he waited with his jaw set, his hand clenched around the hilt of his ornate sword. The breeze feathered his midnight hair off his brow. Nobility shone through his nature, pride intrinsic in his bearing, and the sadness etched in the worry lines around his mouth made her long to reach out across time to offer consolation.

"I guess they just don't make men like they used to. Otherwise, I might not be so damn lonely tonight."

Dana squirmed lower, nestling into the comforter, as her hand wandered over the smooth material of her pajamas. Her book lay forgotten on the bedside table.

"What would a man like you do with a woman like me?"

* * * * *

The fiery nymph on display in her luxurious bed made up for at least twenty of the boring years Conn Hennessey had spent in a dusty attic, covered with a canvas tarp. Her beauty staggered him. Her long legs, spread apart directly in front of him, granted him clear access to admire her freshly waxed mound.

Sweet gods! The need to take her, to consume her, tormented him. Doomed to observe, his eyelids refused to close as manners required. Forced to watch, Conn couldn't even relieve his own arousal as his body demanded. Nine hundred years of torture had taught him any attempt to move was futile. No matter how badly he longed to wrap his hand around his throbbing cock, his arm might as well have been made of steel. It would not budge. The roar of impotent rage bubbling within him would never break through his mouth, forever sealed in that nasty grimace of shock and outrage.

Dana stared straight into his eyes as she inched the shiny material of her garment up her supple belly, innocently setting him ablaze. Her innate sensuality distracted him, pulling him from his fit of anger. Resigned to his fate, Conn admitted the situation could be worse. Her earlier phone conversation had been muffled by the partially closed door. The dread building inside his heart as he listened to Dana's extended grooming ritual subsided now that he realized she hadn't been arranging a tryst with a lover.

Though she'd never brought a man home for sex in her bed, she indulged in occasional affairs. Conn lived vicariously through the steamy stories she related to him about her limited sexual experiences, always devising ways he could have improved her pleasure. He stored memories for the long and lonely times when nothing happened, when his owner deserted the house, leaving him with nothing to occupy his mind. During those stretches of unbearable quiet, he fantasized about what he would do to her if only he could.

On nights like these, when she pleasured herself, his frustration with being denied the ability to delight her became tempered with thankfulness. Her solo exhibition spared him the pain of witnessing another man touching the woman he loved.

She unknowingly teased him by reaching under her gown to cup her full breasts, keeping them hidden from his hungry gaze. Conn wished he could be the one to give her satisfaction.

I'd suck your ripening nipples right through the slick cloth of your nightwear.

A faint whimper escaped her parted lips as a delicate fingertip soothed the peak he imagined his mouth over. It happened sometimes. Maybe desperation played tricks on his mind, but it seemed as if she could sense his thoughts when the emotions running through him boiled up enough, or when her mental barriers were relaxed enough—such as when she dreamed or became intoxicated.

The desire churning inside him flared to white-hot levels of passion when she reached across the mattress to draw a realistic imitation of a cock from her nightstand drawer. Smug pride filled him. He could give her so much more than the merely adequate toy.

If you weren't a godforsaken painting.

Dana flung the silky nightdress off the edge of the bed, her lissome figure now completely exposed to his stare. She lay back, rubbing her delicate pink pussy lips with one hand as she notched the tip of the vibrator against her tight opening.

"I want you inside me," she whispered to him.

You can have no idea how desperately I want you, my lady.

Conn watched the flushed mouth of her pussy contract, hugging the lucky instrument of pleasure at the first glancing contact. Her abdomen flexed and her spine arched as she rose up to meet it. She ran the crown of the buzzing tool across her slit as though relishing the anticipation.

Take it inside you now but think only of me.

Slowly, she pressed the vibrator against her wet entrance until it began to sink inside, bit by bit. In his mind, Conn groaned, remembering how the first flash of slick heat would smother his cock. Even nine hundred years couldn't obliterate the memory of a sensation that powerful.

Feel me inside you, parting your flesh, making room for all of me.

Dana stroked the shaft into her tight channel, picking up speed as she lost herself in rapture. The mewling cries she made aroused him as much as the sight of the broad head burrowing deeper inside her moist sheath on every return thrust. The fingers of her other hand skimmed over her breasts and stomach before dipping lower to paint glistening circles around her clit.

Her muscles gathered tighter as she approached climax. He knew her reactions intimately, having been forced to observe her pleasuring herself many times over the years. Just a few more long, steady strokes and she would come apart.

Come on, sweetheart. You're almost there. Clench around me. Feel me stretch you, stroke you deep inside.

Dana's eyes remained locked on his as she shattered. In that moment, the bond they shared swelled, pulsing with the magic of her orgasm. In his core, he imagined he could sense an echo of her pleasure, though fond memories alone probably accounted for the tingling rush. He accepted the knowledge of her release as the sweetest form of satisfaction—the only satisfaction—he would ever have again.

CHAPTER TWO
All Hallow's Eve, Five p.m.

"I'm in here." Dana called out groggily to Jenny when a key rattling in the front door woke her. She shook her head to clear the clinging remnants of sleep before forcing herself to abandon the arousal still coloring her skin from the intense fantasy she'd been ripped from.

"Hey, what are you doing in bed? You're not bailing on me, are you?" Jenny's inquisitiveness stemmed from concern, not a fear of attending the occasion alone. Her friend possessed an infamous independent streak.

"No, I'm actually looking forward to getting all dressed up. I just took a little nap."

"Are you blushing?" Jenny teased. "Did I interrupt a steamy dream?"

Dana laughed. "You know me too well. Lately, it's getting worse."

"You've been living like a saint. It's no wonder you're all hot and bothered. Maybe tonight you'll meet prince charming or an astronaut or maybe even a superhero! You know, I've always had a thing for Batman..." Jenny continued her gabfest from the bedroom while Dana scrubbed the last of the sleep and the sexy dream from her eyes with water cold enough to shock her system.

When she left the bathroom, a wash of air puffed across her

damp face, identical to the caress she'd felt the night before. Searching for the source, she pivoted, coming face-to-face with Conn—the man who'd made love to her in her fantasy a few minutes earlier. A tingle raced up her spine at the memory.

"Hey, Jenny, is there a draft in here?"

Her friend paused in the closet doorway, holding the garment bag containing Dana's dress in one hand. "Nope. Feels the same as always. Don't try to distract me either, I want to know who you were getting sweaty with in your dream."

Dana couldn't suppress the urge to glance at the painting.

"Him! Again? I mean, he's incredibly sexy but he's been dead for nearly a thousand years, if he was ever alive at all. Can you at least go for someone attainable?"

"I'll try tonight. I'm really in the mood to have a good time."

Dana unzipped the bag her friend held then withdrew the jewel-green, floor-length dress. Gram had modeled the gown after one depicted in a painting they'd seen at the local museum's traveling exhibit on Celtic lore. Fabled to have been worn by an irresistible fairy princess, the costume radiated charm and sexual power. Flowing fabric shimmered with embroidered gold vines and Celtic knotwork that swirled around the deep V-neck and tapered waistline. Her arms would be covered with gossamer panels threaded through metallic golden bands—a shimmering spiral wound around her upper arm and a matching one encircled her wrist—the fabric draping in between.

"Who wouldn't be in the mood for a good time wearing a dress like that? I'm jealous. Your gram really knew what she was doing."

Dana smiled through the emotion clogging her throat. The dress was the last thing her gram ever made. She could still hear the pride in the old woman's voice when she revealed the gift.

"When you're my age, you don't have time to beat around the bush with false modesty, girl. All my life as a seamstress was made for this moment and this dress. There is magic here. I felt it as soon as we saw that painting in the museum a few years ago. I knew it would be the one. This is a dress of dreams. Wear it and remember to follow your heart."

Of course Gram had always been an eccentric romantic and, by that stage in her illness, a lot of what she talked about had been confused, bordering on delusional. Dismissing her wilder claims became second nature as Dana spent time with her during those final weeks. But tonight, it really did seem like magic.

"Jenny, do you ever think there's more to All Hallow's Eve than candy and costumes?" Dana wondered out loud.

Jenny dismissed the thought with a wave of her hand. "Don't be getting superstitious on me. I don't believe in all that hocus-pocus crap. It's an excuse to sell Ouija boards and have some fun. Now let's get it in gear or we're going to be late. I want to take some extra time with your hair and makeup. We're not letting this dress go to waste."

* * * * *

Conn observed the pair gather their purses and other womanly paraphernalia before heading out the door in a whirl of glitz and laughter. Then the clank of the pipes and the drip of the leaky kitchen faucet provided the only reprieve from silence.

Again.

Unfortunately, he knew the answer to Dana's earlier question beyond a shadow of a doubt. Magic surrounded them. The world had undergone drastic changes in all his years as a silent watcher, doomed to observe but never interact. People of this time distanced themselves from the forces of nature with their gadgets and creature comforts, but real sorcery still existed.

How else could I be here still, trapped on this damn canvas?

The sickening dread returned as he imagined Dana's night out. After her recent confessions of loneliness—not to mention the comment she'd made to Jenny about wanting to have some fun—the odds favored another man touching her tonight. How could anyone resist something as stunning as his woman in that magnificent dress?

Conn loved her more with each passing day. As a precocious child living with her grandmother following the death of her parents, she'd entertained him with her lengthy monologues detailing her adventures, her sharp wit and the awareness she seemed to have that he was more than a simple portrait.

As she developed into a beautiful young woman, he found himself longing for her company, to discuss his viewpoints on

14

their one-sided conversations, to reassure her during the awkward stages of youth or to simply laugh with her when she watched the comedy shows she preferred on television. But on her eighteenth birthday, when her grandmother passed the painting to her, he'd truly fallen in love with her.

The first time he witnessed her passion had indelibly marked his soul. From that moment on, he'd acknowledged they should have been mates. Conn couldn't understand how it had happened, but their interests, personalities and passionate natures formed a perfect match. The most painful realization had come not when he understood that sharing a life with her would be impossible but when the nature of their circumstances had swamped his soul with horror. He would be doomed to watch her brilliant inner charm fade and be destroyed by the persistent march of time like so many of his mortal owners before her.

Conn didn't know how he would bear it. He only wished for her happiness in the terribly brief life she would have.

While he should have been satisfied that her solo performance of the night before would not be repeated, that her needs would be fulfilled, he couldn't contain the jealousy budding inside him. Some cocky bastard, inexperienced but arrogant as he had been ages ago, would take her. Some man who couldn't possibly appreciate her as he did would make love to her. And he damn well better make it good for her.

"Or what, Conn, you will hunt him down to go medieval on his ass? Is that not the phrase of today's youth?"

The lilting feminine voice shocked him. No one expecting an answer had addressed him in hundreds of years. It would take far longer than that, however, to make him forget the sweet laughter veiling the darkest evil he had ever encountered.

Deirdre.

A wavering specter floated in front of his fixed gaze.

"Will you not say hello, darling?"

"Witch." After eons of silence, hatred mingled with elation as he relished the ability to croak even one word. "What are you doing here? You're dead, I saw you perish."

Deirdre's somber face, etched with lines of stress and sadness, looked like suffering incarnate. It served her right. After trapping him, her pride had insisted she keep him like a macabre trophy. He observed her mature then rage at the loss of her physical beauty before dying as a reclusive, wrinkled hag in the only moment of triumph Conn had known since she destroyed him out of spite.

"That is not your concern. The time has come to test your true nature…and hers as well. The stage is set, everything is ready. How will you use your time, by lashing out at me?"

He questioned whether solitude had finally annihilated his sanity when the witch's image sputtered and faded in front of him. "What do you mean?"

"Today the veil between the worlds of living and dead, magic and mundane is thinnest. She owns your heart already. Now you need to complete the circle."

"Damn you, Deirdre. What do you speak of? Will you allow me to leave here?" He couldn't keep desperate hope from coloring his voice.

"You'll have until the end of the spirit phase to convince her of your love. If you cannot earn hers in return by midnight tomorrow, you'll be banished into the painting, alone forever."

"Why are you doing this? Haven't tortured me long enough? Release me. Let me live in peace." Conn didn't notice the heat at first. Anger saturated his senses, obscuring the subtle tingling in his feet until it built into the world's worst case of pins and needles.

"I'm sorry. Magic works by its own rules, is limited by forces we cannot control." The witch faded further, transforming into a glimmer of light and motion. "This is all I have left to give. Make it count."

The burning expanded from his legs, engulfing his torso. As the sensation intensified, Deirdre dimmed until only a hint of her figure was visible and the scratchy whisper of her voice barely reached his ears. But he couldn't ignore the irony of her parting words.

"Conn, I never meant to hurt you."

Before he could process her final comment, he stumbled from the frame. Stiff joints thwarted his attempt to make an agile leap in front of Dana's bed. A loud crash reverberated through the room when he dropped to his knees on her dresser, scattering perfume bottles and knickknacks, before toppling forward onto the floor. The plush carpet, though much more luxurious than the standard dirt from his time, was not quite as soft as it had appeared from his perch. The fibers mashed into the side of his face as he lay stunned, staring under the frilly dust ruffle ringing the base of Dana's bed.

Dana! The entire exchange had altered his life in a few brief seconds, but any hope of breaking the curse of the painting would be lost if he allowed her leave to depart for the party and spend the night without him. Time slipped past. Every movement of the second hand on her bedside clock clacked as loud as thunder in his spinning head as he struggled to wring movement from his limbs. Muscles creaked with disuse, bones cracked and joints popped, but he managed to shove himself up and take a painful, staggering stride toward the front door.

Conn thanked the last several owners of his painting for placing him in rooms with either radios or TVs. The past hundred years had armed him with the means to assimilate the changes in technology and culture in the world. Otherwise, simple things like unlocking the door or buzzing himself out of the building might have cost precious instants.

His determination to catch Dana propelled him down the stairs, despite the cacophony of sound and motion surrounding him, in time to watch her settle gracefully in Jenny's car. Even with the benefit of TV, viewing the future firsthand instead of through a small moving picture astounded him for a moment. So many buildings, so many people, and everything moving so quickly disoriented him.

Free motion began to return to his limbs, whether spurred on by fear of losing her or due to some lingering magic, Conn didn't know or care. He bolted past the luxury sedan parked on the curb to a taxi whose customers were just exiting. Climbing in behind the driver, he pointed to the sleek black automobile rolling away, merging into traffic, then shouted, "Follow that car!"

The driver chuckled, "Buddy, you watch too many movies."

Conn utilized the trip into the country to organize his reeling thoughts. Emotions threatened to overwhelm him as he wrestled with the excitement, disbelief, desire and even fear coursing through his veins. Nervous energy kept his body in constant motion—fidgeting in the backseat of the personal vehicle—

refusing to stay still after being stationary forever. Even his curiosity at experiencing a ride in an automobile for the first time couldn't distract him from the much bigger issues at hand.

Questions zoomed through his mind like the scenery that whizzed by outside the window, but one truth was universal. Magic or not, he wanted Dana Kavanagh with an intensity surpassing his wildest fantasies. But now that he could actually possess her, cruel fate permitted him only a few brief hours to accomplish his goal after centuries of waiting. To him, thirty hours seemed like a flash of lightning or the blink of an eye.

As the cab rolled through the intricate iron gates of Jenny's family estate, he realized some form of payment would be required. Jenny's car stopped under the covered portico near the garages while the taxi swung into a round drive near the front entrance to the house. An elderly man in formal attire, whose job description included handling situations exactly like this one, opened the door of the taxi. All the years of listening to Jenny share stories of her family with Dana was about to pay off.

Conn exited the taxi, hand extended, and addressed the older man by name. Nerves threatened to discredit his performance but too much depended on success for him to fail now. After all, he'd been a dignitary himself once. State affairs had posed no challenge for him then. Diplomacy, charm and resourcefulness had been second nature.

"Good evening, Gerald. I'm Conn Hennessey, the escort Jenny arranged for Ms. Kavanagh tonight." He faked a self-conscious chuckle as he glanced down at his outfit. He was clothed in the same garments he'd been wearing the day the witch stuck him in the painting. "She wanted me to match Dana's costume—not what I would have chosen myself, of course. It seems I've left my billfold in my street clothes. Kindly take care of the cab for me and I'll settle up with Jenny later."

Before Gerald had a chance to object, Conn moved toward the portico, but the women had vanished. Apparently, even that brief exchange had provided enough opportunity for them to make their way inside. He rushed up the marble staircase to the grand front entrance of the mansion, glad to see his appendages had regained most of their motor control during the hour-long drive.

How hard could it be to find one person?

CHAPTER THREE
All Hallow's Eve, Nine p.m.

Dana danced, laughed and chugged liquid fortification, hoping to loosen up enough to find a man to share the night with. She lectured herself about being too picky, about sabotaging the plan, but so far, she hadn't found a meaningful match. No matter how much she wanted to, she couldn't be like Jenny. She needed more than a living, breathing dildo to be satisfied. Dana could only sleep with a man she felt something for, someone who attracted her.

She dismissed the cowboy, after he practically tried to ride her on the dance floor, with a kind but firm refusal, making it clear he didn't interest her. With every man she eliminated from the running, a new one appeared.

It must be the dress!

It acted as a hottie magnet, drawing men like moths to a flame. Attractive men—including a fireman, a gunslinger, a surfer and an Indian chief sporting a loincloth that left nothing to the imagination—expressed interest in making this a night to remember. The attention that had gratified her at first now edged toward stifling. Her wallflower tendencies won out over the spotlight starlet she was made up to resemble.

Before the gorgeous man in camouflage made good on the promise in his eyes, she escaped out the rear exit of the glass solarium where most of the guests partied. The music hushed as soon as the thick door swung shut behind her. She drew in a lungful of cool air, relishing the scent of leaves and smoke from the small fire pit at the end of the patio. Several tables and wicker sofas spread across the area, lit with jack-o'-lanterns, where a smattering of couples lounged, getting acquainted in the more subdued atmosphere.

She wandered to the far edge of the outdoor space, sighing as she admitted she couldn't stand to go inside for another round of auditions. A one-night stand wouldn't cure her recent restlessness, otherwise she wouldn't be running from every eligible man who touched her. Lost in thought, she didn't hear the footsteps until they stopped right behind her.

Maybe if you don't turn around, he'll go away.

"Dana?" The rich voice surrounded her with its rustic accent.

She turned, expecting to find someone familiar, although she couldn't place the unique lilt that sang the two brief syllables of her name. But what she saw startled her.

"What! Is this some kind of joke? Who are you?"

"Sir Conn Hennessey at your service." His broad hand reached out for hers and she automatically took it. His heated fingers drew hers to his mouth. A soft kiss brushed his moist lips over her knuckles before he murmured, "Enchanted to finally make your presence, ma'am."

"Did Jenny put you up to this?" Her voice resonated with the incredulous cast of her thoughts. Down to the rich brown tunic and intricate sword she had studied on many long nights, Conn Hennessey looked identical to the man from her painting. Dana tried to focus on his answer but she couldn't ignore the flash of desire blossoming in the pit of her stomach. A fantasy come to life waited before her. Attraction flooded her senses.

"No. I'm afraid not." He grimaced. "Are you certain you're well? You look somewhat pale."

The trembling in her legs intensified until she feared she might fall. He took the glass from her hand, saving her from sloshing wine on her dress, then braced her next to his side and lowered her to the wicker loveseat, sheltering her under his arm.

"Here now, I'm sorry to have startled you. I didn't consider how you would react to the sight of me." He murmured soothing apologies, granting her time to absorb his presence. Patience paid off, lulling her, especially combined with his broad hands rubbing up and down her spine. "I was afraid I'd missed you. I've been looking for you for hours."

"Where did she find you?" Her voice sounded dazed even to her own ears.

"Who?" His hand stilled in its circuit on her shoulders.

"Jenny." Dana retreated from the intoxicating warmth of the man's body to study him now that her heart rate had slowed from hypersonic to merely accelerated. Her hands extended, as if they had a mind of their own, and she skimmed her fingertips across the planes of his face, over his eyebrows, his high cheekbones, his strong jaw and even his full lips. "It's amazing. You look just like him. I mean, you look just like the man in a painting I own."

The cerulean ice of his eyes shone even in the dim lighting. His coal-black hair flopped over his forehead, waiting for a breeze to stir it off his face, exactly the way the artist had captured it. The only difference between the man in front of her and the image she'd memorized over the years stemmed from this man's lack of anger. It softened his features from harsh to unbearably handsome.

"Perhaps that's because I *am* the man from the painting."

"The details are perfect. She must have taken a picture sometime…" Dana's rambling drifted off as she continued her explorations. The elaborate design of the stitching on his sleeves drew her gaze along it to the scabbard at his side. She traced the raised pattern of metal and gemstones reverently, admiring the craftsmanship necessary to forge such an extraordinary replica.

"Don't fret over the details, my lady. Sometimes the simple answer is best. Let me give you this night." His azure eyes implored her to throw caution to the wind and surrender to the sparks of attraction fizzling in her blood. "Can you pretend I am your liege from the wood?"

The rise and fall of his theatric voice reminded Dana of old movies. She wondered if he practiced the cadence and antiquated inflection as part of his disguise. If so, his appearance here tonight couldn't be a last-minute setup. A lot of thought and planning had gone into this performance. In a way, the gesture touched her like all gifts that held meaning for their thoughtfulness rather than their intrinsic value.

22

She remembered her gram's words then... *Follow your dreams.*

"I'll try, if only to find out who put you up to this."

Conn handed her the half-full glass of wine she'd been nursing before he found her. "Finish your spirits. Then I'd like to walk with you in the moonlight."

Jenny had obviously arranged to give her a dream for her birthday. The attraction shoving Dana toward the man in front of her would be ludicrous to deny. Her panties had already dampened between her thighs. Only a romantic would have agreed to fulfill her fantasy, which counted as a mark in his favor. Who was she to ruin a lot of effort on both their parts, when she wanted the man anyway?

"All right, Sir Conn Hennessey. For tonight, I am yours."

Conn bundled two wineglasses and a full bottle of merlot in one of the tablecloths he filched from nearby. He tucked the fabric under one arm then took Dana's hand with the other. The first contact with her satiny skin nearly caused him to roar in satisfaction. He focused on subduing the trembling in his limbs, unwilling to risk frightening her away with the intensity of his reaction.

She twined their fingers together, comfortable with his touch but oblivious to the significance that one simple act held for him. He felt alive and real, grounded by her recognition of him, truly believing for the first time that he wasn't fantasizing.

They headed along the winding stone path into the well-manicured grounds. Enthralled by her company after so much time alone, and unused to talking aloud, he must have let the silence linger outside of Dana's comfort zone. Tension seeped into her arm. He rubbed his thumb over the delicate spot between her thumb and first finger, quelling her skittishness.

"My apologies, *mo shearc*, it's been so long since I had a companion that I'm afraid I've lost my manners." He shook his head then clenched his jaw. Once, his charm had been legendary among women.

"It's been a long time for me too."

The hesitancy in her voice almost made him laugh, but he didn't care to offend her. Dana couldn't comprehend the disparity involved. He'd meant nine centuries, not nine months. Of course she wouldn't believe the truth yet. If it hadn't happened to him, he probably wouldn't believe it either but, somehow, he had to convince her the curse existed.

Conn lectured himself on the necessity for restraint. She believed she accompanied a stranger, but reserve seemed impossible around someone he knew so well.

"We'll go slow," he vowed, though denying he intended to seduce her would be futile since he'd already begun to do so. "For now, just be with me. I believe you understand what it means to have someone to talk to."

The promise came easily despite the lifetime spent craving her, because hurting her or frightening her would only pain him double. He could be tender.

For now.

She'd attended the party tonight in search of someone to ease her loneliness. That, combined with his certainty of their compatibility, made him confident the evening could have only one outcome—as long as he didn't scare her away with the intensity of his pent-up need.

Her face turned up to him, silhouetted by the moonlight. She looked like a goddess. Her red-gold curls sprang full and wild, framing her delicate oval face. The milky-white skin above her neckline and on her arms glowed with vitality in the dark. His hungry eyes devoured her attention and he prayed for the control necessary to play this game despite his frantic urge to touch her, to feel her around him, knowing he may never experience the sensation again after these two days were gone.

Some of the desperation flogging him must have colored his expression because Dana picked up on it right away. Her sensitive nature was one of the things he admired most about her. She guided the conversation as deftly as he navigated their way along the moonlit path, handing him the opportunity to confide in her as he so badly wished to.

"Okay then. Talk to me, Conn. Tell me about the painting. There are so many things I've always wondered. Who was he? What was he doing there? Where was it? And mostly, why is he so angry? So hurt?" Dana rested her head against his shoulder as they strolled along the walkway, the night sounds of crickets and tree frogs surrounding them. She was only playing along, trying to distract him from the sadness she read in his soul, but he wanted to tell her the truth.

So he did.

"I was born into a powerful family. My father spent his life trying to bring peace to our people, halting the fighting that had infested our land for centuries. His largest rival agreed to unite our two clans through marriage. As the eldest son, I was to wed his daughter—a beautiful, powerful witch. As soon as I received word of the initial proposal, I knew it would eventually be decreed by our fathers. Therefore, I sent word for her to meet me in the forest, in the clearing depicted in the painting."

Dana loved stories, she read constantly, and this one seemed to be no exception. As he spoke, they reached the end of the trail near a wide pond. A gazebo stood on point, stretching out over the water. Still weaving his tale, he led her inside.

"Her name was Deirdre. We met every day for months in the clearing, attempting to acquaint ourselves before our families negotiated the official bargain. We both agreed it would do nothing for our cause if we couldn't commit our souls to each other. A loveless marriage would only fester, generating more tension between our people. I cared for her. I found her alluring and intelligent, but I didn't love her."

Conn removed cushions from the benches lining the edges of the circular structure then constructed a mattress on the floor with them. He spread the tablecloth over the pallet then invited Dana to get comfortable with a wave of his hand. She relaxed on the fluffy pile, leaning forward to remove her sexy high-heeled shoes. He couldn't help but admire the dark valley between her breasts. She glanced up, waiting for him to continue, and he had to drag his thoughts to his place in the account of his life.

He huffed out a sigh. Having centuries to mull things over had altered his point of view, but the end of his story still filled him with the pain of shock and betrayal. "The time neared when our families would mandate our union. I still did not love her. I never would, not in the way she needed. So I left, intending to tell my father I could not marry her. However, she believed *she* loved *me*. She became enraged. She lashed out with her power, trapping me in that damn painting."

Without realizing it, Conn had sunk beside Dana. They lay next to each other on the impromptu bed. He reclined on his back, allowing her to come to him on her own though he wanted to devour her, claim her. She draped casually over his chest, fitting into every rise and fall of his body in absolute perfection. Absently, he trailed his fingers along the length of her curls, taking solace in her nearness and acceptance. Even the slightest touch made a banquet for his starving senses. The weight of her head on his shoulder, her luscious breasts pressing into his ribs, and the whisper of her breath on his neck threatened to overwhelm him.

Conn could see every instant of his fateful meeting with Deirdre as though it were happening all over again. Only this time, he could commiserate with the fear and frustration she must have experienced. The perspective terrified him.

What if Dana cannot love me in return?

"Now, nine hundred years later, she's finally let me free. But only for tonight—All Hallow's Eve—and tomorrow." Their foreheads touched. The words he shared fell into the intimate hush surrounding them. He stared into her eyes while he told her the truth. "If I can't convince you to love me, she's going to banish me forever. It will destroy me. I can't return now."

From where she rested on top of his solid chest, enjoying the pastoral harmony of the evening and the heat of the man next to her, Dana burst out laughing. Her giggles simply refused to be contained any longer. She buried her face against his shoulder, completely at ease with him, and let herself enjoy the wonder of his company.

"Would you shut up and kiss me already?" His head came up off the cushion to look her in the eye, but she saw no hint of amusement there. "God you're good. I don't know how you kept a straight face through the whole thing. But I think a fable that entertaining deserves a reward."

His pupils dilated as the intent of her statement became clear.

"You will allow me to love you?" His breath feathered across her lips, a hairsbreadth apart already.

"Well, I wouldn't want you to be doomed forever. I don't think I could live with that kind of guilt on my conscience." Her amusement bubbled up again as she thought of the crazy, romantic fairy tale he had spun without effort. She might even have started laughing again if he hadn't leaned forward with a groan, sealing his mouth over hers.

CHAPTER FOUR
All Hallow's Eve, Ten thirty p.m.

The first caress of his lips as they nudged hers freed blinding desire from Dana's soul. Sir Conn Hennessey, actor or not, intrigued her. The man who would indulge her fantasy, building it up instead of tearing it down to make room for his own needs, had captured her heart in an instant. The chemistry that had grown more potent with every step they had taken along the garden path tonight burst into an inferno of lust.

His hand trembled in time with the fluttering of her heart as he levered onto his elbow, forcing her to lie back while he cupped her cheek in his palm. Her eyes were open, watching desire turn his glassy as he delved deeper, flicking his tongue between her slightly parted lips. His every movement displayed expert technique, arousing her with subtle, precise strokes of his tongue, nips of his teeth on her bottom lip and the restless movement of his fingers massaging her scalp before they buried themselves in her hair.

His face rose up from hers even as she stretched her neck to keep him from breaking the sweet contact. For a moment, he read her expression before groaning. Through the supple fabric of her dress, the hard ridge of his erection made a prominent ridge against her belly.

"You're so beautiful, *mo fiorghra.*" His brow rested on top of hers as he nuzzled his cheek against her own. His touch worshipped, so careful and delicate, as though she were a china plate that might break beneath him. He drove her crazy, aching to grind herself against him, make him touch her fully. Nothing in her life before had been as sensual as these small gestures from him, especially when coupled with the evidence of the need he controlled. It built between them, pressing like water on a dam until she crumbled under the weight of their desire.

"More, Conn. I need more," she moaned in his ear when he bent to lick and nip her neck. Dana guided his much-larger hand to her breast, squeezing over top of his, trying to soothe the heaviness settling there.

"Slowly, little one. I don't want to hurt you. Savor every moment." Passion made his words husky, more seductive, enhancing the lilting timbre of his voice.

"I am. I promise. Please, please just give me more." Dana's petition astonished her. A sexual yearning more intense than hurricane-force winds blew through her body, overpowering reason and logic. Bone-deep lust caught her off guard, considering she'd met this man less than two hours ago, but he seemed custom-designed for her alone. Everything from the way he smelled, like spice and earth, to his tender yet fierce embrace signaled perfection to her instincts.

"Shh…" His lips brushed hers as he whispered against them. "You don't know what you're asking for, my lady. Let me take you at my own pace." His hand slid from her breast to her abdomen, spanning her waist from hip to hip. The warmth from his palm soaked through her dress as he petted her. The caress meant to soothe only stoked the flames higher though, and she undulated helplessly beneath his sensual assault.

She opened her legs wider, accommodating him as he settled between them. They moaned in unison when his engorged erection nestled into the valley between her legs, perfectly aligned to press against her clit as she continued to move in sinuous arcs beneath him. His head dipped once more, kissing her with increased fervor while one hand untied the halter knotted behind her neck. She began to shrug out of the coiled fabric and armbands winding around her biceps, but his other hand encircled her wrists, pinning them above her head.

"Leave them. They're beautiful. You look amazing like this."

Conn lifted his chest from hers without breaking the contact of their mouths stroking each other. She captured his tongue between her lips and sucked it with bold pulls as he peeled the front of her dress off her torso. The cool breeze of the night air coming off the water rushed between them, pebbling her nipples further.

Without looking, Conn reached down and found the distended peak with unerring accuracy. His fingers moved as though he knew every inch of her intimately, making the exploratory groping of a first-time lover unnecessary. Sharply honed instincts must have guided him, leading him to touch her in the way she craved and even inventing sensations she'd never experienced before.

Dana buried her fingers in his thick, silky hair as he bent to lick a tightening spiral around her right breast. He teased her without mercy, coming oh so close but not quite touching her nipple. She attempted to tug him over the peak, crying out for his attention, but he resisted—continuing to torture her with anticipation.

"You're so sweet, Dana. I love the way you melt beneath me." The vibrations of his compliments, spoken against her flesh, sent a current of desire straight from her chest to her crotch. Her muscles clenched, forcing viscous fluid from her channel.

"Conn." She gasped his name when his lips enclosed the tortured tip of her breast in their warm wetness. He alternated flicking his tongue over one while his hand played with the other, kneading the flesh that overflowed his fingers. Hovering over her, supported on his knees and one elbow, his free hand worked the fabric of her dress lower until she had to lift her hips for him to slide it, along with her silk panties, from under her ass with one swipe of his hand.

When she attempted to touch him, stroke him in return, he refused then trapped her hands above her head again until she stopped struggling. "I won't last if you touch me, *mo shearc*."

His kisses spread farther across her belly and hips. He lingered over her navel, rimming the depression with his tongue while his chin pressed tantalizingly close to her clit until she cried out for more. Shifting, he peered up at her face. His mouth hung so close to her bare, slick mound, every harsh breath he took rasped against her needy flesh.

"Tell me you want it," he commanded, his eyes fixed on hers. "God, yes. Please, Conn. Taste me." Instead of the fluttering butterfly kisses she expected by now, he dove right into the moist folds of her sex without hesitation as though he would devour her. Pleasure erupted along her nerve endings, stoking the fire inside her to a conflagration of ecstasy. The tip of one large finger sought the entrance to her soaked vagina, teasing her but not entering. Her labia felt swollen and deprived.

Dana drew her feet up onto his shoulders, granting him free rein to do with her what he pleased. Such a skilled lover, someone who allowed her to rely on his knowledge of her desires and guaranteed he would fulfill them, someone who encouraged her to be completely open was a treat she'd never sampled before.

Conn ran his free hand up the outside of her thigh, patting her as he continued to work her slit. Desperate to be filled, she thrust her hips at his circling finger. The first knuckle notched into her, poised to penetrate. Dana cried out as the intensity of her pleasure built toward orgasm.

"You taste so good, little one. I don't want to stop feasting on you but I know you're ready to come for me, aren't you?" She moaned her assent. "I want you to shatter, on the first stoke of my finger within you—the first miniscule entering of my body into yours."

His strained voice alerted her to the fact that giving her pleasure drove him nearly mad with excitement. It pushed her into the whirlpool of ecstasy, sucking her deeper under his spell.

"Now!" she yelled, oblivious to their surroundings or the possibility of anyone overhearing her passionate cries.

Conn drove his blunt digit inside her all the way while his lips simultaneously closed around her clit, sucking gently. As he commanded, she exploded over the edge into orgasm, clenching around the long, graceful implement impaling her. He continued lapping at her with tender strokes as she finished riding the waves of pleasure before withdrawing his hand. She watched, dazed, as he slid it into his own mouth and ingested the proof of her surrender.

Her body still hummed with arousal, greedy and unsatisfied after her earth-shattering release. Dana gaped as he stripped off his clothes. His body gleamed in the moonlight, statuesque and tall. His cut figure made her hands and tongue yearn to trace every ridge and crevice of his muscles, though nothing made her ache as bad as the sight of his cock rising proud from the dark hair surrounding it.

Conn's erection stood, bobbing against his abdomen in time with his pounding heart, the head leaving a glistening trail of pre-cum that reached onto his six-pack abs. Dana had never seen anything more magnificent than the picture this man made sitting on his haunches between her legs, watching her with genuine concern.

"I'm afraid I won't be able to be gentle, *mo shearc*. I've never wanted like this before."

"Then don't be," she whispered. "I want to feel your passion, know you want me enough to make you lose control. Do it. Fuck me, Conn. Just…"

He swiped his thumb over the spot on her lip she worried with her front teeth.

"What is it?"

"There's a condom in my purse if you need one."

"But you take birth control pills, correct?" His forehead creased.

Of course, Jenny must have told him. Her friend would have insisted on all medical checks if she thought things might come to this. The practical business had her scrambling to reclaim the illusion, which had wavered at the reminder of their game.

"I am," she moaned. The thought of taking him naked made her ache to have him buried to the hilt. "I haven't been with anyone in a long time. I'm clean."

"I swear the same."

"Then take me. Please."

Dana adored the feral glint in his eyes as his restraint shattered. In one fluid movement, he scooped his hands beneath her, raising her hips, aligning his steel-hard shaft with her pussy. They both monitored the junction of their bodies, a moment away from paradise. A flash of doubt made her tremble. His hard-on would be the largest thing by far she'd ever taken inside her.

Then their eyes met and she whispered again, "Fuck me."

With a guttural shout, he buried himself several inches in her tight pussy with one stroke. The shock of suddenly being full to bursting stole Dana's breath away. Conn covered her, lying heavy on her chest, struggling to give her time to adjust. Breath rushed into her lungs in a huge gasp, driving her wild. She bit the side of his neck, silently urging him to take her.

Bracing himself on his forearms, which bracketed her face, he began to thrust inside her, using her ample arousal to coat his shaft and tunnel into her farther with each advance. His smooth motion rubbed the base of his cock across her clit with every powerful stroke. No words were necessary as they gazed into each other's eyes.

Dana moved in tandem with him, enhancing his movements, fusing their bodies more completely as she met his hips on each stroke until his heavy balls rested against her. She howled her possession, cushioning his entire length inside her. Together, they increased the tempo of their thrusts until they became a sweaty bundle of motion and slick, slapping, sucking sounds.

"*Fiorgrah.*" His soulful call made it clear the term of endearment addressed her. "I'm going to release. Inside you. Finally. I need to feel you shatter around me."

All she could do was moan in response. The slippery walls of her pussy constricted, each ring of muscle acutely aware of the passing of his thick, powerful shaft stroking in and out, harder and faster. Her fists balled on his back and her toes curled as she strained against him.

"Come with me, Dana." He practically growled his demand. The raw lust in his tone dragged her over the edge. He slammed his cock fully inside her, grinding his pelvic bone against her clit. As she shattered beneath him, he cried out, a sound hauntingly desperate, completely honest. "*Mo fiorgrah.*"

With that one word, his cock swelled inside her, growing longer and harder than the moment before when he already stretched her impossibly. The pulses of his release traveled up his thick length, rippling the flesh impaling her. The hot blasts of his cum splattered against her sensitized tissues. The evidence that she pleased him so immensely set off another cycle of spasms stronger than the last. She climaxed as he filled her with his semen, her muscles milking him dry.

They collapsed together on their makeshift bed, recovering their breath, content to hold tight to each other and listen to the splash of the fountain in the pond, the crickets chirping and the frog's song as the night fell quiet once more.

Contentment suffused every fiber of Conn's being, threatening to overwhelm him. He anchored himself by wrapping the woman he loved in his arms, a precious gift he never dared even to hope for. The fact this amazing experience followed a sexual release of epic proportions nudged this instant as close to heaven as he thought possible. He dreaded moving from this spot, afraid to break the spell, but Dana shivered in his arms. The stroking motions of his hands on her cool flesh beneath the tablecloth wrapped around them no longer kept the chill night air from seeping into her.

"My lady, it's too cold for us to stay out here all night." He pressed his lips to her brow before untangling their limbs and the yards of fabric from around them. He drew the sheer golden material and jewelry from her arms where it had started to unravel after their vigorous lovemaking.

"Don't wanna go." Dana's eyelids drooped in a slumberous gaze. She sounded sated and groggy as she tried to nestle into the pile of cushions.

He knelt beside her, affectionately tracing the edges of her satisfied smile with one finger, drinking in the sight of her lying before him as he rose to draw on his clothes. He stared into her eyes, hoping she could not deny the truth in his own. "I wish this night could last forever."

"Mmm... me too."

Conn wrapped the wine, glasses, their shoes and his sword in Dana's magnificent dress and his tunic before handing her the bundle. "Hold that for a moment."

Smug pride had him grinning when she accepted it without hesitation, too sleepy to question him. He draped the edges of the sheet around her before lifting her and their belongings into his arms. Still intoxicated, whether from the alcohol or their passion or both, she snickered in delight before snuggling closer, dropping her head onto his shoulder.

"Where are you taking me?" Her playful question made him smile.

The relaxed mood and his obliterated barriers led him to answer without thinking as he made his way toward the structure a short way down the path. "To the stables we passed on the way here. It should be warm enough in there. The building looked better constructed than even the most luxurious homes of my time."

She stiffened instantly in his arms. "Who are you really?" she whispered.

He faltered, his steps slowing momentarily as he considered his response. The short window before the end of the holiday didn't leave room for anything but the truth if he intended to break the curse of the painting. Praying to every god he'd disavowed over the centuries, he hoped Dana could handle it.

"I'm the man from your painting." He reaffirmed it as gently as possible, hoping to soften the shock of the words.

She squirmed in his grasp, attempting to break free from his hold, but he only hugged her closer. When she spoke, the pain in her voice cut him too. "Is this a game to you?"

He stalled a few feet short of the barn door. "Look at me." When she didn't obey, he shook her a little more harshly than he intended. "Look in my eyes, *fiorghra*."

Dana swallowed hard, her delicate throat flexing beneath pale, pale skin, but she raised her face in brave defiance until she peered into his eyes without flinching.

"This has been the most extraordinary night of my life. No matter what tomorrow brings, I need you to understand that nothing could be more important or more serious to me than what's happening between us right now." He projected the conviction burning all the way to his soul.

She focused on his declaration, weighing it, judging his sincerity.

"I believe you." Her sigh leaked all the tension from her body. He wished she believed his story about the painting but would settle for the truth about his emotions for now.

Conn nudged open the door to the barn with his shoulder, kicking it shut behind them. The interior glowed with a soft light someone had left on in the tack room. He stifled the urge to inspect what appeared to be prime horseflesh and equipment, instead heading for the loft. He set Dana on a bale of hay while he gathered supplies—an electric lantern and several clean, soft horse blankets.

When Dana shed the tablecloth to help him create their cozy nest, unselfconscious as she worked nude, Conn nearly dragged her straight to the plywood floor. Splinters be damned. She bent to spread and fluff the hay before layering on the blankets, exposing her hot pussy to him. In that moment, the perfect words fell from his mouth before he could stop them.

"Come back to me."

Her spine straightened so fast, he feared she might slip.

"What did you say?" She glanced over her shoulder, trying to see him clearly in the dim light.

"You heard me." He debated playing it off, as though he didn't understand the significance of what he'd said, but he couldn't. "Come back to me."

The heat in his eyes must have made her believe he just wanted to go another round. When she pivoted, he drew her in close to his body. Her skin warmed again beneath his fingers. He stole a deep, drugging kiss before their conversation went further, in case she threw him out.

She smiled when he parted his lips from hers slowly, lingering. "It's funny, for a minute I thought you were quoting a movie."

"I was. *Somewhere in Time*. It seemed appropriate given our situation."

Dana sat heavily on the bed of hay and blankets she'd finished constructing. "It's my favorite movie."

CHAPTER FIVE
All Hallow's Day, One a.m.

Dana shivered as Conn stalked closer. He draped his leggings over their other clothes before settling in beside her. They sat on the crude mattress, their shoulders resting against a bale of hay. Her emotions wavered between the elation that stemmed from their perfect date, even excluding the best sex of her life, and the trepidation rising in her that this hoax he perpetuated would cheapen the experience. Because, if his acting skills allowed him to persist in this charade, then how could she trust the emotions she thought they were sharing?

"I guessed as much. You must have given it a dozen viewings this year." He sounded utterly genuine when he asked, with just the right amount of concerned interest, "Why do you always cry when you are already aware of how the story ends?"

"If you were really the man from my painting, you would know the answer to that question." Dana wrapped one of the blankets around her, tucking her knees to her chest and folding her arms over them. She laid her head on her arms, staring off into the darkness outside the loft window.

"I think it's because you eternally hope for a happy ending. I think it's because you wish love were enough to bring someone through time. I think it's because you love me even though it's irrational and you thought it impossible we'd ever meet." His hand cupped her cheek, turning her to face him. "But I want to know."

"If I tell you, will you stop this act? Obviously, Jenny compiled some big, fat dossier of facts on me for you. It was fun at first, flattering that you'd both take so much time, but it's starting to creep me out." She attempted to keep the disappointment from her voice but failed. Despite his earlier claims, he couldn't be interested in a relationship beyond this night together if he wouldn't tell her about his real identity.

"Please answer. I will only be honest with you, I promise." He plucked her hand off her knee, enfolding it in his reassuring grasp.

She nodded before glaring at him from the corner of her eye. "Okay then, but the truth is pretty pathetic. Don't you dare laugh at me."

"I would never mock your heart, little one." His fingers squeezed hers, encouraging her.

"I cry every time I watch that hokey old movie because I believe every person has one soulmate and, for most of my life, I've dreamt of the man in that damn painting. I'm afraid I wasted my chance at happiness by loving a figment of my imagination more than I'll ever be able to love an earthly man because, in my mind, he's perfect. I feel complete when I talk to him and my fantasies are so damn real that I can't imagine giving him up."

Dana's eyes burned with tears, alarming her. For the first time in her life, she'd admitted a secret to someone before first sharing it with Conn. The real one. A betrayal in some ways, it also relieved her. Maybe hope existed after all.

"I'm surprised you haven't run away, thinking I'm nuts, or at least obsessed, by now," she laughed. A harsh, deprecating wheeze shattered the stillness of the barn.

Conn tugged her into his lap, cradling her in his embrace. He kissed her eyelids, licking away the tears clinging to her eyelashes. "Any man would be lucky to be the object of your affection."

He continued touching her, igniting the flame within her all over again. Their physical attraction didn't surprise her since he so closely resembled Conn, but his tender understanding and graceful acceptance of her fantasy made her fall a little bit in love with this man, wherever he'd come from.

Dana wound her arms around his neck. She buried her face against the taut muscles of his chest, afraid to look in his eyes when she begged, "Make me believe, Conn. Make him real tonight."

"Yes, my lady, follow your dreams." His strong hand cupped the nape of her neck, his fingers stroking her, as he whispered in her ear. "Remember what your gram told you when she handed you that beautiful dress right in front of me. You were always meant to be mine."

The sultry declaration aroused her as much as his wandering touches, which skimmed the tops of her breasts. She listened to his heartbeat accelerate with her ear pressed to his chest. Dana couldn't resist the urge to touch him, taste him. She turned her head, laving his pectoral muscle, savoring the tremor that ran through him with the first swipe of her tongue.

"Yes." The word was a hiss as he guided her mouth to his nipple. "You have no idea how many nights I watched you lying in bed and imagined your sweet lips on my flesh."

Dana groaned as she envisioned her artwork transformed into a voyeur. Conn settled her between his knees. She shed the blanket, revealing herself to him fully. Leaning forward, she continued the trail of kisses across his rock-hard abs, pausing in wonder to trace each enticing line of his body. And still he kept talking, never stopping, though his voice became strained with the effort.

"*Mo fiorgrha*, you're amazing. I would see you playing with that sweet pussy and wish that I could be the one to bring you pleasure, not some piece of plastic or even your own fingers." He gasped as she sank lower, her lips a hairsbreadth from the head of his engorged cock. His hands fisted in the hay behind him as his breath sawed in and out. Dana smiled while he struggled to keep himself still—giving himself over to whatever she chose to do to him.

"I knew that with the right man your passion would be unstoppable. Gods, you have no idea how badly I yearned to be that man. The one to guide you, teach you how to please me and show you all I could give you in return." As Conn spoke, a bead of shiny cum leaked from the tip of his hard-on. She couldn't resist. Her tongue lashed out, swiping the moisture from the slit cupping it. His salty, musky flavor thrilled her while his shout of pleasure encouraged her to take more.

"When you slept, I felt your soul open to mine." His tortured growl begged her to continue, or to believe him, both of which she did in the magic of this moment. Dana wrapped her hand around the base of his erection then eased her lips over his cock. She took him inside her mouth, inch by inch, until her lips met her hand and he pressed into the back of her throat. "In your dreams... I showed you...what I wanted."

He struggled to speak. His tense muscles quivered with the effort it took him to stay calm. She recognized without direction exactly how to please him. He'd given her the key. Her vivid dreams contained details she never would have thought of on her own, her sexual experience being limited in real life. She'd always assumed those sensual details came from her subconscious desires leaking through, but what if they had really been a gift from him?

Dana cupped her other hand around his balls, weighing them in her palm as she massaged them. Above her, Conn groaned, trembling beneath the strain of staying motionless as he let her explore on her own. She loved the way he stretched her mouth, so large, hot and hard.

Her hand and mouth moved in synch, stroking as much of his skin as she could. His scrotum drew close to his body, preparing for release. The rush of arousal surprised her, priming her to join him. The gratification she brought him radiated through her. Her creamy arousal wet her thighs.

"Enough, little one." His raspy command drew her gaze to his. "I need to be inside you again."

Already in motion, Dana released his cock with a pop as he reached for her shoulders. He turned them around, flinging a blanket over the bale of hay now in front of them. The pressure of his hands on her shoulders followed until she knelt in front of him, bent at the waist, the top half of her body sprawled across the cotton-covered bale of hay. Conn's shaft bumped her pussy as he crouched behind her.

"Are you ready for me, *mo shearc*? You're so small, so tight." When he ran his hands over the length of her spine, she thrust her ass at him, inviting him to wedge inside and stretch her. His cock bobbed and teased her clit as he rubbed it between her pussy lips with slow, teasing glides.

"Please, Conn, fuck me." She needed him now. Dana reached behind her, trying to guide him to her, but he captured her wrists in one hand and held them in the small of her back, trapping her in place on top of the hay.

"Wait for it, little one." He smoothed the head of his cock over her slick, sensitive labia, nudging her clit. She couldn't bear the sweet torture. Instead, she squirmed, hoping to force him to impale her.

His other palm landed on her ass cheek with a sharp crack, startling her. The resulting burn shot straight to her core, driving her desire higher as the sting fizzled to a warm glow.

"You like that, don't you?" he whispered in her ear as he bent close, rubbing the heated spot on her ass with his abdomen.

"Yes, more," she begged. Conn nipped her neck before rising up again. He spanked the other side of her ass until heat tore through her veins. She arched her spine, presenting herself like an offering.

"You were meant for me alone, Dana. Say it. Tell me you're mine." He shifted his hips, notching the head of his cock in the center of her moist folds. Sparks of pleasure erupted in her brain, making it impossible to speak. His open hand connected, harder this time, as need drove them both to the edge. "You're mine, *fiorghra*. Mine."

"Yours. I'm yours." She cried out as he thrust inside her with one powerful stroke, embedding himself balls-deep. The force of him spreading her clenched muscles nearly sent her over the edge right then. "Fuck me. I need you."

Conn's roar overflowed the loft with power and compulsion. His thrusts were desperate and vigorous, lacking the finesse he'd demonstrated in the gazebo earlier. With her wrists bound behind her, she couldn't brace herself. The arc of their bodies rasped her chest against the covered hay, the tempered sensation on her nipples like tiny pinches or a lover's teeth.

With every plunge, his sac slapped against her clit. Wetted by her juices dripping onto them, coating them, they glided across her sensitized bundle of nerves, caressing the point of her pleasure over and over.

He filled her so full she feared she might break around him. Wild with lust and longing, she lost herself in the moment. Dana's engorged walls grew tense, squeezing him tighter, making him force his cock home with lunges that guaranteed he stroked her with his entire shaft.

"That's it," he shouted. "Clench around me, come for me."

The pressure built until she couldn't resist it any longer. She surrendered to the shattering release, coming around him. Her pussy gripped him, spasming so hard she thought he might never get free.

Behind her, Conn bellowed a moment before the jets of his cum flooded the cavern where she cradled him. Still the contractions continued in the longest, strongest orgasm of her life. She couldn't breathe through the pleasure swamping her senses. The stars she saw as she exploded faded to darkness.

Conn gathered Dana's limp body into his arms. He laid her on the pallet she'd made before cleaning her, using tender dabs with a corner of the tablecloth. He dared to hope for the first time they might be able to unlock the curse together. How could she deny what they had shared tonight?

Only two souls in love could meld with such perfection.

Utter contentment surrounded them as he settled beside her then drew her tight to his side. For the first time in nine hundred years, Conn Hennessey closed his eyes to sleep.

CHAPTER SIX
All Hallow's Day, Ten a.m.

Dana opened her eyes after another one of her dreams of Conn. Only this time, it wasn't a dream. Sunlight streamed through the loft window, casting golden beams and shadows across the landscape of his torso. She studied his features while he slept. He looked totally at ease lying on the floor of the barn, hay sticking to his rumpled hair.

They look exactly alike. What if it's true? What if he really is Conn?

She wanted to believe it. Last night would remain in her memory as the best night of her life. How could she have shared that kind of intensity with a stranger?

He knew things about her she couldn't remember telling anyone else. Maybe she'd confided in Jenny about her gram's speech when she'd given her the dress, and sure, Jenny knew about the dreams of Conn but only in a vague way. Dana had never spilled the details to anyone.

Conn could have guessed some things about her, such as her tendency to cry over sappy movies. She wasn't sure, but his sincere intensity had started to convince her last night.

"Good morning, *mo fiorghra*." His eyes still hadn't opened but awareness radiated from him.

"What does that mean?" Pretending to be asleep served no purpose.

43

His sky blue eyes peeked out from beneath heavy lids as he decided whether or not to tell her. "My true love."

"I don't understand this."

"All you have to know is what you feel for me and what I feel for you." He drew her hand to his chest and pressed it over his heart. "I love you, Dana Kavanagh."

The sexy man in front of her dropped those three words like a bomb on her life.

"I'm not ready! I'm sorry. This is crazy. I can't fall in love with someone after a single night." She sounded panicked even to herself.

He sat up calmly. "I understand, Dana. This is quite sudden. Get dressed. Let me take you home. We can talk. I'll tell you anything you want to know. Just give me a chance."

* * * * *

Dana entered the mansion, thankful for the lighter mood Conn had shared with her on the walk to the house. He'd left her at the door with a sweet kiss then went in search of a ride home while she ran inside to use the restroom and scrounge some breakfast.

In the bathroom, she examined herself in the mirror. Her face heated, adding to the redness of her swollen lips and the small abrasions where the hay had scratched her face. The spots, not to mention her disheveled hair and clothes, acted like a badge that openly declared her romp with Conn.

Hoping she could avoid any of the other guests still lingering about, she snuck down the hall. Her luck ran out when she rounded the corner. Brian, Jenny's brother, lounged against the granite kitchen counter, his arms crossed over his chest.

"There you are." His suggestive smile left no doubt he noticed the signs of her romp in the barn. "Would you call my sister already? She's been bugging me every half-hour, wondering where you are. I let her suffer. I hope she's worried sick after this stunt."

"Sure, Brian. Sorry if I caused you any trouble. Thanks for the party last night. I had a great time." Dana scrambled toward the door, breakfast forgotten in her discomfort. His uncharacteristic hostility surprised her. She'd even imagined he was attracted to her on occasion.

"I just bet you did." The short burst of laughter grated on her nerves. "If I know my sister, she sprung for the best."

"What's that supposed to mean?" She turned, unable to prevent herself from challenging him. Tales of his sexcapades traveled far and wide. How dare he criticize *her* for taking one night of pleasure?

"Shit, baby, you didn't have to stoop to this. I would have fucked you for free."

The air whooshed out of her lungs. She lurched as her stomach dropped to her feet. She blinked. "Wh-what?"

The thread of sound barely broke free of her swollen lips.

"Oh damn, you didn't know?" The shades of disgust in his eyes turned to remorse. "When your man got here last night, he told Gerald my dumbass sister hired him as an escort for you."

"She *paid* him. I-I thought it was a blind date..." A lance of pain shot through her.

"Yeah. I'm sorry, Dana." He reached out to steady her but his touch repulsed her. She felt dirty. Reeling from the news, she tried to evade his grasp.

"Take your hands from her." Conn's command echoed cold and hard as he stepped between them, breaking Brian's hold. "What's happening here?"

"The game's up, asshole." Brian puffed out his chest, clearly intending to attack. Dana had only seen the man act so protective once before, when someone had threatened his sister. "I let Dana in on your little secret."

"What in the hell are you talking about?" Conn refused to submit, still shielding her from Brian. His stance kept her locked in the corner of the kitchen, unable to flee the room.

"The fact you're a man-whore." Brian's laughing sneer got to Conn. He lunged forward, slamming Brian against the wall.

"I am no such thing," he snarled in Brian's face. The two men struggled, muscles straining for superiority.

Brian slipped an arm free then used it to swing at Conn's head. Conn ducked in time to avoid most of the momentum but a glancing blow clipped his temple, momentarily distracting him. Brian took the opportunity to knee him in the stomach.

Conn grunted but caught Brian and twisted, flinging him into the cabinets opposite the corner where Dana stood frozen in shock.

Teeth gritted, Brian spat out, "What, you prefer 'prostitute'? 'Gigolo'? Or maybe 'escort', like you told Gerald last night."

Conn stopped fighting immediately. He spun to face her, leaving himself wide open.

"Oh gods. Dana, it is not what it appears."

She studied his face. The panic written in the creases of his forehead and the wild look in his eyes, made it clear he really had done what Brian accused. Her insides crumpled into a knot of pain. She thought she might be sick.

"You made a fool of me," she cried. "I started to believe you."

Conn would have blocked her exit from the kitchen, from the estate, but Brian recovered his breath enough to kick Conn's feet out from under him, slamming him to the ground.

Choked by shock and agony, Dana ran. She didn't stop to answer the questioning calls of concerned guests who spied the tears streaking her face or heard her ragged sobs. Bursting out the front doors, she searched for a way home. She'd nearly made it to the garages when Conn yelled for her to stop. His footfalls pounded on the pavement as he came flying up behind her.

"Dana! Please wait. I can explain."

She grabbed a set of keys off the hook by the door then pressed the panic button on the key fob. Lights flashed on a sleek, silver BMW. She made her way to the car, stumbling and banging her shin on the bumper of another vehicle but she hardly noticed.

Conn grew closer now, nearly to the garage. "Stop! Don't go."

She climbed into the car, but her hands shook so bad she couldn't align the key with the ignition. Conn yanked the door open, his breath heaving out of him in giant pants, but his hand was gentle when it wrapped around her wrist. Dana tried to wrench away but she had no chance of evading him when she shook uncontrollably from her violent weeping.

"You should not drive in this condition, my lady." He relaxed, calmer now that he had caught her.

"I'm not your anything. Leave me the hell alone."

"Let me assist you." He nudged her, pushing and lifting until she half crawled, half fell into the passenger seat of the car to avoid his touch.

She yanked the opposite door handle, moaning when it didn't budge. The child locks must have been engaged, disabling the latch. She should have railed at him, kicked and fought, but the strength leached from her bones. The venom poisoning her, killing her heart and hopes with every beat, didn't affect her speech though.

"What's your fee for driving me home? Do I owe you a tip or is it part of the package?" She sighed, defeated, hollow and distant.

Conn ignored her comment, starting the engine instead of deigning to respond. He seemed to be concentrating on the control mechanisms, flipping the wipers on by mistake then the turn signal, before finally putting the car in gear. Dana slumped against her door, setting herself as far away from him as possible in the confined space.

The car edged from the garage at a snail's pace then lurched over the curb to the walkway.

"*Cac!*" he cursed in Gaelic before overcorrecting and taking out a whole row of flowers.

In the midst of this insanity, her insides like broken glass, all Dana could do was laugh. She laughed until she cried again as Conn made his way down the long, hedged driveway after sideswiping about ten feet of the perfect box-shaped hedge. By the time they reached the main road, he seemed to have himself under control and his driving improved.

"How do we get home?"

"Make a left then follow the signs to N71 North." She ignored the twinge in her heart at his ignorance. When would she remember it had all been a sham?

In the silence that followed, Dana's thoughts raced around her mind.

How could I have been so wrong about him?

"I'd like you to telephone Jenny." His request came soft but stern.

"I don't want to talk to her." She couldn't keep her bitterness from showing.

"Please."

She didn't answer him right away but the longer she debated, the more anger pressurized her.

"Fine. There *are* a few things I need to say to her." She jabbed her finger on the dial button of the car's hands-free system. Punching in Jenny's number, she tried to gather her thoughts from the swirling mass of confusion inside her.

"Dana, is that you?" Jenny answered before it rang.

"Yeah." She could only force out one word past the sense of betrayal that threatened to defeat her.

"Oh thank God! Brian just called, he told me what happened. Are you okay?" Jenny sounded frantic with worry.

"No, I don't think I am."

Conn moved his hand as though to hold hers, but she smacked it away.

"Listen, honey, I think there's been a big mistake. I'm not sure what's going on but Brian was pissed. He hardly ever gets so mad. He said something about me hooking you up last night but I didn't. I swear that I didn't, Dana."

"You mean you didn't *pay* the man who looks like my painting to fuck me?" Dana couldn't help the harshness of her rebuke.

"What!" A pause followed on the line. "Look, Dana, I definitely didn't hire someone to sleep with you! I would never do that. How could you even think that I would?" Dana refused to allow guilt to eat her over the wounded tone of her friend's voice.

"Okay, you didn't give him cash. But you did set me up, right? Who is he, where did you find him? He hasn't even told me his real name!" The admission revived the pain of her shattered hopes, sending more tears over her cheeks.

"Dana, are you crying? Calm down, hon. I didn't fix you up with anyone last night. I definitely don't know a guy who resembles the stud from your painting. Where are you? Can I come get you? I've been sick with worry since I lost track of you at the party last night."

"No. I'm almost home. I just want to be alone for a while." *So I can figure out what the hell is going on around here.*

Jenny agreed reluctantly, "All right. But call me later, okay?"

"Sure." She hung up without saying anything further, her mind already working on the puzzle. "Take the next exit then the second left. My apartment is on the right."

"I think I know what happened." Conn glanced from the road for a moment. His hands clamped around the steering wheel in a white-knuckled grip.

Dana didn't answer. She wished she could turn away and look out the window but the need to see his face, to try to discern the truth from his expression, overwhelmed her better judgment.

"Last night, when I fell out of the painting—"

"Oh come on, are you back to that again?" Sarcasm dripped from her.

"I promised I would not lie to you. I swear that I am not." His proclamation still rang honest. If he lied, he was the first person to ever fool her gut instincts.

"Next thing, you're going to attempt to convince me that you meant it when you said you loved me." Her accusation snapped out with a fraction of the sting she intended. It hurt her heart to remember how she'd absorbed his romantic nonsense like a foolish schoolgirl. Meanwhile, he'd probably been laughing at her for being so gullible.

"I do love you, *mo fiorghra*." Ironically, the words she'd waited her entire life to hear sounded bitter.

"Conn—"

"Don't say anything for a minute."

"Did you just tell me to shut up?" Her hackles rose.

"See, I think that's exactly what happened last night. When I arrived at the party, I had no money. I asked Gerald to pay for my cab and told him that I would settle up with Jenny later. I had to tell him something to keep him from arguing, so I lied. I said that I was there to escort you at Jenny's request. Things must have gotten twisted somehow. In my haste to catch you, I may have worded my tale improperly for today's language."

What he said made sense but believing him had gotten harder. Earlier today she'd acted like a naïve fool. She wouldn't repeat that mistake again so soon. Fortunately, they'd turned onto her street. Another minute and it wouldn't matter anyway. Then she could shove some distance between herself and the humiliation she'd suffered.

"I don't know what happened. I don't know who you are or why you're here. Maybe someone's playing a joke on me. Maybe you're the man in the moon. I don't know. I just need you to leave me alone."

"I can't do that, Dana." He slowed at the curb in front of her building, the front tire hopping up on the sidewalk before he parked.

"Open the door," she demanded. When he didn't respond fast enough, she pointed to the button then hissed, "Press it. Now."

The moment he did, she bolted up the staircase to her apartment. Of course he followed right behind her. "Please let me come in. Allow me to spend some time with you, show you I'm not a bad man."

"No, that's not a good idea." She unlocked her door then slipped inside, careful to swing it behind her, leaving a crack open to whisper through. "Goodbye."

She slammed the door, throwing the deadbolt before sinking to the floor. The *thunk* radiated through to her when he did the same on the other side of the wood panel, dropping his head back. Emotionally drained, she wished things could have ended up like she thought they might this morning. Turning, she kissed the oak with the barest brush of her lips before heading into her room.

Dana couldn't bear to look at the painting. She felt childish but she covered her eyes as she snuck past its spot on the wall to get to the bathroom to avoid the searing pain she knew it would bring. The need to take a shower overwhelmed her. Maybe then she could think more clearly.

CHAPTER SEVEN
All Hallow's Day, Noon

Conn sat in the hall outside the door to Dana's apartment, trying to formulate a plan, but so far all he had was hoping for the best and that probably didn't count for much.

How had everything gone so awry since this morning?

"Well, the miscommunication with your host certainly didn't help." Deirdre's gnarled, haggard form appeared out of thin air. She floated next to him so they stared at Dana's door together.

Talking with her stole precious time from his attempt to prove his authenticity to Dana, but he had several things to get off his chest while he still had the chance. "Hello, Deirdre."

"Good afternoon, Conn. I came to remind you there are but twelve hours left before the window closes and your opportunity is lost."

"Deirdre, I want to apologize for my inability to give you what you needed all those years ago. If I caused you even a fraction of the anguish gnawing my gut, knowing I stand to lose her, then there's nothing I can say or do to atone. I see why you were angry enough to curse me." He reached out to hold her hand but his fingers passed right through her. So instead, he set his on the floor just beside hers. "I also want to thank you for coming to make things right, for trying to help me, even if this doesn't work out."

"I love you now as I did then, Conn, but you still don't

understand me." The sadness in her frown had him blinking.

"What do you mean?"

"I didn't capture your soul in that painting to harm you or because I was angry."

"Deirdre, it's all right. I forgive you." He harbored no ill will toward her.

"I had a vision, months before we ever met. I hoped that it would be false, but I knew in my heart such a strong epiphany was fated. It warned me not to go to the wood or answer your summons. I saw myself lying heartbroken, growing old alone." She sighed then continued.

"The distant future was also revealed to me. Through some slip of fate, you were born out of time. I was shown this woman, your woman, and I knew you were made for each other but had no hope of ever meeting. Every day for the months we shared, I soaked in the joy of your company. It would have to warm my heart forever. By night, I scoured my father's kingdom for tomes of magic that might hold a solution. I hoped every day you could love me, but it was not to be. When we ran out of time, when you had to admit the fondness we shared could never develop, I preserved you. For her. But being young and arrogant, I didn't fully realize the consequences that action would have, the burden it would place on my soul. So much of myself went into that magic. I can't ever move on. I'm tied to it. Here, old, weak and ugly. I'm not certain I could do it again. Not even for you, my lord." The telling of the story weakened her. She flickered and faded.

Memories flashed through his mind. All the conversations Deirdre had with him in those first days after she trapped him…no, saved him. He hadn't been able to listen to what she'd tried to tell him then. He hadn't heard through his rage. All the nights she had cried herself to sleep, alone. Love had driven her to endure them for him. Such an act of bravery humbled him.

"Deirdre, don't go. I've been a fool. Stay with me a little longer."

They sat in companionable silence for a few minutes, each lost in their own thoughts—just as they used to during their days in the forest—until finally he spoke. "How can I repay you?"

"Don't allow my sacrifice to go to waste. Convince her to

love you." Her entreaty dwindled, thready and weak. "Already the power of the day is waning. It is harder for me to come to you like this. You must be ready before midnight or I won't be strong enough to return you both to the painting."

Conn spun to face her. "What do you mean, 'return us both to the painting'?"

Her timeless eyes blinked. "It's the only way, Conn. You'll be forever young, eternally together."

"I thought if she loved me, I would stay here with her!" He sprang to his feet, pacing.

"No, Conn, it cannot work that way. The magic demands a soul." Her image was barely visible. "I will come back. Midnight. Must gather strength."

"I won't do it, Deirdre. I won't damn her to a life like I've had."

But he shouted at nothing.

* * * * *

Dana finished her shower, feeling no better about the situation. Maybe she would try to sleep for a while. She dreaded going into her bedroom. Seeing the man she dreamed about would always be painful now. Her anger over having her fantasy stolen from her nearly outpaced her hurt over the lies Conn had told her.

How dare he say he loved me?

She stomped into the bedroom, determined to prove she could face him without flinching, but something crunched beneath her heel. Bending to investigate, she discovered the contents of her dresser scattered across the floor.

What the hell?

She plopped backward onto the edge of the bed. Then she noticed the mess on the floor. It radiated out from the spot directly below the painting as though something or *someone* had fallen out of it, scattering the items on top of the dresser below.

She inhaled a fortifying breath before turning, but even that couldn't prepare her for what she saw.

He was gone.

The painting hung, unharmed, in its usual spot on the wall.

Only, instead of a portrait of a man on a horse, the artwork's subject consisted of a horse in a wooded landscape. She recognized the copse of trees in the background. The setting had not changed, the man was simply missing.

Dana sensed the difference. The indefinable spark that had intrigued her had vanished. The absolute emptiness of the room surrounded her but her mind still had trouble accepting the truth. *Holy shit. This is not what it looks like. Think!*

Would someone be cruel enough to go to these lengths to trick her? For what purpose? If getting her to go on a date was the intent of the sham, then why mess with her room after she left?

On shaking legs, Dana retrieved a chair from the dinette then dragged it to the dresser. She could tell for sure if someone had forged a replacement. She climbed on the furniture then used one finger to separate the edge of the frame from the wall until she could peer behind it. Sure enough, a faint scratch on the bottom right-hand corner resembled a shaky *D + C* enveloped in a rough heart. No one could fake her six-year-old handwriting well enough to dupe her.

No one would know to look.

"Conn!" she screamed for him, realizing the extent of her mistake.

I have to find him!

She sprinted for the front of her apartment, oblivious to her near nudity in the thin silk bathrobe. When she flung open the door, he stood right outside the threshold, ready to knock on her forehead. Before she could settle on what to say, he beat her to it.

"I thought of something that will convince you." His subdued reaction surprised her, something had changed.

"No—" She started to protest. She already believed him.

"I'll prove it to you." He shouldered her aside, his eyes momentarily blazing when he caught the gap in her nightgown. She belted it as he stepped inside, refusing to be distracted.

She tried again to interject, to explain what she'd found in the bedroom, but he shushed her by laying his finger over her lips.

"I recall something you would never have shared with anyone." He tugged her closer. "When you were sixteen years old, one of Gram's customers came to pick up his alterations when she was not at home. He became angry and you knew she couldn't afford to lose his business. You told him he could wait." Once he started the gruesome account, she couldn't stop him. Dana needed her suspicions about that day confirmed. The telling obviously hurt him as much as it scared her to remember. The lines of tension built around his mouth and eyes, transforming his face into the mask of anger and outrage familiar to her. In that instant she couldn't have denied the man before her was Conn, even without the initials in the frame, even without the horror he recounted for her now.

They moved closer to each other, drawn together by shared memory, each reliving *that* day. Dana stroked his arm in an attempt to calm his rising unease.

"The moment he looked at you, I knew trouble brewed. I struggled in vain as he slid closer and closer on that couch, encroaching on the space you attempted to put between you. I couldn't stand the thought of him hurting you while I stood by and did nothing. By the time he touched your breast through your shirt, anger consumed me."

Despite the time and distance, Dana still shivered hearing Conn's recollection.

"When you fought him and he still persisted, I thought I would erupt with fury." Shockwaves of his emotions rippled through her even now.

"You got so mad the light bulbs shattered," she whispered.

"I thanked the gods when I saw the glass stuck in him alone." He kissed her face, a million tiny touches of his lips across her skin.

"I convinced myself it was a freak accident. But I think I always knew, Conn." She stretched up on tiptoe to drag his mouth to her. She consumed him, giving him all the pent-up love and desire she'd kept in reserve when she thought him an imitation of her fantasy.

He withdrew to stare into her eyes. The wistful tone of his voice made it clear he hardly dared to hope for vindication. "Then you believe me?"

She nodded. "And I love you, Sir Conn Hennessey."

Conn crushed her to his chest. He devoured her lips as he walked her toward the bedroom. His hands flew under her robe, stripping it from her shoulders. It fluttered to the ground around her ankles. She knelt to work the fastener at his waist while he shed the tunic. In ten seconds flat they fell together onto the plush comforter topping her bed.

They lay on their sides, facing each other. The delicate sweep of his fingertips skimming across her arm, waist and hips contrasted starkly with the desperation of his mouth claiming hers. His strong body seared her hands. The sinewy muscles of his back rippled as she explored. The curve of his ass shaped her palms as she dragged him closer, craving his rigid shaft sandwiched between them.

Conn groaned. His hips arced reflexively, rubbing the length of his cock over her. She wiggled until she had one leg thrown over his hip. Her pussy clenched as his shaft rode the furrow between her thighs, stroking her and spreading the wetness that oozed from her pussy on every pass until he glided silkily between her legs. Still their mouths mated, tongues caressing and thrusting inside each other's lips.

His hands roamed lower on her back, tracing the cleft of her bottom, making her shiver. Conn clenched her ass cheek in one hand, his fingers splaying into the crack to tease her higher. She rotated her hips, trying to align the head of his cock for entry. He smacked her behind, making her squirm in his hold, only driving her passion higher.

"Not yet, little one. I want you to scream with need first." His growl vibrated her lips, punctuated with a nip on the lower one.

"I'll do whatever you want, just fuck me. Please." She needed to be filled, to revel in the pressure caused by his large member forcing its way through her tight sheath.

Instead, he spanked her harder. The flash of pain and pleasure spurred her on and was no punishment at all. Still he wouldn't give her what she craved. She threw her weight forward, pinning his hip with her leg—already draped over it—until she lay on top of him.

"I want your cock inside me now." Dana rose with her arms locked straight in front of her, palms flat on his chest. She rocked her hips over his straining erection in short strokes, causing the bulbous head to rub wet circles around her clit. Reaching behind her, she cupped his sac in her hands, teasing the center fold with the tip of one finger. "Can I have what I want, Conn?"

"*Mo fiorghra*, you can have anything. Take it. Take me."
Now *he* begged *her*.

Her hand traveled upward after one last, lingering stroke over
his balls to encircle the base of his cock. She rose above him,
making room for his flesh to stand poised to enter her as she
hovered over it. Slowly, Dana lowered herself onto the tip. The
sense of power overwhelmed her as she studied his expectant
expression.

Conn's hands wrapped around her hips, supporting her
gradual descent. He didn't try to force her or rush her but held
her suspended until she sank lower and took him inside.

"Not too fast, little one." He moaned. "You're so small. I
don't want to hurt you."

Dana lifted, sliding until his cock lodged barely inside her,
then dropped suddenly, taking as much of him as would fit. They
cried out together. His hands cupped her breasts, easing some of
the weight there. He used the globes to draw her near until his
lips could capture the peak of one in his warm, silky mouth.

Her hair curtained them. Conn's hips bucked beneath her
when the strands brushed his chest. She sucked in a breath,
urging him deeper than ever before. Sitting astride his trim hips,
she swore his cock pierced all the way to her soul.

"I've always longed for your magnificent hair on my body,
mo shearc. So fiery, so beautiful."

He resumed sucking her while she shook her head, dragging
the curls over his torso. The pressure inside her eased enough
that she began to move over him, using his tense lower abs to
manipulate her clit. The contact caused her to clench around him,
hugging his cock. It twitched as his muscles contracted in
ecstasy.

"Yes." His pupils dilated as he lifted his head to peer between
them, to witness how completely he tunneled inside her. Dana
rode him harder, thrusting in longer strokes while grinding her
clit on his pelvic bone on every downstroke. "That's it, fuck
me."

She threw her head back, spine arching, and impaled herself
on his thick shaft. The plump head nudged a sweet spot when he
couldn't help but move while watching her abandoned display.

The pleasure grew until contractions began in her slick channel. He raised his feet so his knees bent, providing support for her back.

"Put your hands on my knees, little one." Conn guided her, still completely in control despite their positions. She did as he instructed, using the leverage to force herself on him harder, faster, deeper. Dana's arms behind her thrust her chest forward like an offering, which he eagerly accepted, pinching her nipples with enough force to sting.

She bit her lip, concentrating on the angle of penetration, aiming the head of his cock against the front wall of her vagina. Sparks shot through her when she hit the perfect spot and screamed out his name. He rocked his hips, repeatedly stroking the sensitive area on her swollen tissue. Each pass of his shaft over the area brought her closer to release.

"Come for me, Dana."

They pressed together once more, their bodies in perfect alignment, causing her to fly over the edge into orgasm. When her pussy spasmed around him, she thrashed in his supportive hold. She would have collapsed onto his broad chest if Conn hadn't flipped her to her back.

Conn covered her entire body, skin to skin. His large frame swallowed her petite one as he wrapped around her like a living vine. His arms folded over her waist, cradling her close, and her legs circled his hips, locking them together. With a moan, he seized her mouth with his, tangling their tongues as intimately as the rest of their bodies.

Dana's system recycled the pleasure still seeping through her as Conn began to rock into her. After no more than a handful of devastating strokes, the pleasure multiplied, even stronger than before. He drove into her with long, smooth glides. He teased her mercilessly, pulling completely out, leaving her empty and aching, before plunging in balls-deep.

"Harder, Conn." She begged for it and he responded. He pounded into her, strong and sure.

"I'm not going to last." A light sheen of sweat built on his forehead and chest, making his skin gleam.

"Don't go easy…want it," she panted.

In a frenzy of movement, his passion broke free. Conn

slammed into her. Their bodies slapped together. His balls striking her ass sent vibrations up her spine. He nestled lower so their chests massaged each other. The rasp of his lightly haired chest on her nipples caused her pussy to tighten. His heavy presence cocooned her in his warmth as his cock shuttled within her.

"Dana! I love you." His shouted declaration accompanied his orgasm. They shattered together, his cock pumping her full of his cream even as she exploded around him.

In the stillness that followed, she stroked his hair while he lay heavy on top of her. She relished the euphoria before whispering, "I love you too, Conn. Forever."

Following the phenomenal sex, Dana would gladly have drifted off for a nap, snuggled close to the man of her dreams, but he refused to relax completely.

"What's wrong, Conn?" she asked him, dreading the answer. The perfection of this moment should not be tainted.

"Nothing, *fiorghra*." He snuggled close, but the nervous energy she picked up from him started to rub off. She grew restless, her mind spinning in new directions.

"Conn." She rose up off his chest to look at his face.

"Yes, my lady." He smiled but it seemed sad.

"If you've been in the painting all this time, how did you know how to drive?" she wondered.

"It was a little rough there at first. Obviously, knowing how and actually doing it are two different things. I've seen enough TV to learn about a variety of subjects but, from now on, could you play me some action movies once in a while instead of all the girly stuff?" he teased.

"You can pick whatever you want." Her mind reeled, cataloging all the things he'd never experienced. "God, Conn, there's so much you probably want to do. We can travel if you like, see the world. I don't have a lot of money but I'm careful. I have enough saved that we can manage a few things."

Conn didn't answer.

"There's so much... What's your favorite meal? I could cook for you right now. We could order delivery if you want to try something new or go out to a restaurant."

"Dana, that's enough." His unexpected harshness cut her. Her excitement had prevented her from noticing the subtle change in his posture until he interjected. "We need to talk."

CHAPTER EIGHT
All Hallow's Day, Three p.m.

Conn hated himself when fear replaced the giddy excitement in his lover's eyes. He tossed the fluffy blankets to the floor then slunk from the bed.

"*Cac*, Dana. I am not sure how to say this." He paced now, back and forth.

"Say what, Conn?" Dana sat up, tugging the sheet with her like armor against his news.

"I can't stay." The suffering on her face mirrored the wound on his soul. To have a taste of her only to have it ripped away surpassed all imaginings of cruelty.

"I... I don't understand. You said that if I loved you, you would be free." He watched her eyes fill with liquid agony. The sight broke his heart. "You don't want to be with me?"

He crossed the distance to her side in one long stride. "Shh. That's not the problem, *mo shearc*." He picked up her hand and held it to his heart. "I will always love you, remember? I would never choose to leave you."

"Then what's changed?" Her innocent eyes bore into him like lasers cutting to the truth.

"I have." The stormy look clouding her face warned him of her impending fit of anger. "Don't go any further, Dana. It's not what you think. I've changed for the better and it's because of you."

"So, you're saying it's my fault you can't stay?" He loved the fire in her spirit that prepared her to battle.

"No. What I'm saying is that I didn't realize the implications of the curse sooner because I didn't understand true love or the things it can make you do. I didn't understand Deirdre or her motivations."

"So, maybe now would be a good time to fill me in on your revelations."

Conn accepted the bitterness in her tone. It wasn't really directed at him.

"Deirdre was always quite vain. She loved to be told how beautiful I found her. I remember now how she fought against the passing of time. As she grew older, she tried to concoct all kinds of potions to slow aging in order to keep her superficial beauty, but she couldn't outrun time. Eventually it wore her down, as it does everyone. She suffered. I'm ashamed to say now that I didn't care at the time. Part of me enjoyed her pain." Conn sighed and wondered what might have been different if he had understood her better all those years ago. Probably nothing.

"I still don't get why you can't stay, Conn." Dana had quieted, her agitation replaced with fear.

"Because, when she doomed me to that painting, she thought she was giving me the greatest gift of all. Eternal youth." Disgust rolled through his gut as he thought of the hell he'd suffered for nine hundred years. How could that be a gift? But Dana, always sensitive to the feelings of others, understood right away.

"She would've thought it better to be captured forever young than to age and die after a full life. So...you can't stay here but I could go with you. Into the painting." Her faraway gaze and her teeth worrying her lower lip proved she considered the possibility.

Conn grabbed her by the shoulders. "No, Dana. You can't. I won't let you."

"Who gave you the power to decide my fate, Conn Hennessey?" She twisted beneath his hands, breaking his hold.

Panic rose in him. "I won't allow you to throw your life away! You can't understand what it's like in there. You can't move, you can't talk, you can't laugh or dream or make love. Nothing. *Cac*! Don't you understand? I wouldn't even be able to see you if you stood next to me."

Dana leaned forward, cradling his head against her breasts. "Okay. It's okay, I do understand." The promise held no sarcasm or anger. She truly did comprehend the consequences.

Conn's faith in her as the strongest, most amazing woman on earth proved well-founded when she said, "So, let's not waste our time together then. What would you like to do with the next eight and a half hours?"

* * * * *

Dana waited for the delivery man to bring their meal while Conn drew a bath. His list of activities ranged from adorable to sentimental to downright naughty. He kept the content of the latter category of suggestions a secret for now.

So far they'd surfed the internet to uncover history on the lives of his family, finally fixed the leaky faucet in her kitchen, which he said drove him nuts, ridden bicycles around the park, found a building downtown with an elevator he could try—plus fool around in—and dashed through a sprinkler despite the cold November air.

Next, he wanted to explore the wonders of indoor plumbing in a steamy, hot bath. It sounded like heaven to her as she stood shivering in her damp clothes. No matter how hard she tried, Dana couldn't help glancing at the clock every few seconds. The red display on the stove seemed ominous, glowing nine o'clock already. She didn't want to ruin the terribly brief time she had left with Conn by mourning, there would be time enough for that later, but something niggled at the recesses of her mind.

What if…

The doorbell rang. She dashed to answer it, check in hand. As Conn's meal of choice—Dana tried desperately not to think of it as his last meal—he wanted pizza. Fine by her, she would indulge him in anything he desired.

She put the pepperoni slices on her nicest plates, grabbed a bottle of wine and went to serve him. He stood in the water, lighting the remaining candles around the far side of the tub surround. Dana shed her wet clothes, taking the opportunity to admire his naked form while he finished. Then he took the plates, set them on the windowsill and held his hand out to help her into the tub.

"You're cold, *fiorghra*." He kissed her briefly before settling into the water. "Come, sit with me. This is marvelous."

"Mmm. It's one of my favorite things on earth." She submerged herself until the water covered half her chest. Conn looked over at her hungrily, but right then her stomach growled. Loudly.

He laughed in delight. "I'd forgotten what it's like to truly exist. I'm starving. Let me try this pizza everyone seems to love. The commercials for it made me miss eating more than you can know."

Conn ate his pie then stole most of hers as well. They drank the wine and joked until they were pleasantly full. Reclining together, the effects of the alcohol, soft lighting and warmth lulled them into a satisfied daze.

"You have to try one more thing before the water gets cold," Dana suggested from her place lounging against his side. "Press that button to your right."

He turned on the jets, playing with the controls until they swirled at her favorite setting, forceful but not blasting. Conn held his hand in front of them, testing the strength and the pattern of the flow.

Then he turned to her with a devilish smile. "So what is it you do in here that has you moaning loud enough for me to hear in the other room?"

Dana blushed. "Umm…"

Conn laughed as he teased her further. "Do you put your pretty pussy in front of this current and let the water roll over it?"

"Maybe." She didn't resist when he lifted her into his lap.

"Let me watch you please yourself with it," he whispered close to her ear. The dripping arm he banded around her waist held her secure as he positioned them both until the current washed over her clit.

"Right there, little one?" He shifted beneath her, jostling her from the perfect spot.

She pouted in complaint, a whimper escaping her throat, but he soothed her.

"Wait one second. I will make it better for you." He fulfilled his promise by lifting her high enough to slide her over his erection an instant later.

She gasped as he stretched her. He spread their legs, lining her up with the jet once more.

"Yes, Conn. You make me so full." His balls floated up, bobbing against the entrance to her pussy where the water that caressed her rushed over him too.

"This feels so good, *fiorghra*." He bit her neck gently, his other arm reaching around to massage her breasts. "Stay still, little one. I don't want you to move at all."

Dana complied, lying as limp in his arms as she could make herself. The lack of motion only enhanced the clenching of her pussy around his cock. Every tensing of her muscles felt like a full feast of motion. The water swirled around her clit and his testicles, driving them both higher.

When her head lolled onto his shoulder, their gazes met. He lowered his head to hers, kissing her with torturous, slow movements of his lips. Conn licked the seam of her mouth, biting and teasing her, dodging when she tried to intensify the contact. He pinched the nipple cupped in his hand hard enough to sting. Her pussy clenched in response, making them both groan.

The pleasure rose in her until she couldn't restrain her hips from thrusting against his, moving his cock within her. His arm clamped around her like a seat belt, restraining her.

"No, little one. I want you to come from just holding me inside you. Squeeze my cock tight. Hug it with your sweet pussy." She did as he requested, finding the rewarding sensations more intense. "Good girl, now I want you to squeeze it three times then rest."

After triple bursts of pleasure, the temptation to continue egged her on, but he shifted away from the jet. "No. Only three at a time. Start again."

She greedily took the opportunity, doing as he told her. The moment of rest contrasted the intensity of her squeezing around him, preventing her body from growing accustomed to the sensation. Every pulse of tension he allowed flashed through her senses.

"Yes, yes, that's the way." His cock twitched as the fisting of her muscles affected him as well. She was so close now, reaching for the precipice.

"Keep your rhythm, *mo shearc*." He let her complete the cycle a few more times, her ecstasy overtaking logic before he informed her, "You'll come when I count to three."

She moaned, all her muscles straining with the effort of keeping still while the water seduced her. At the start of the next batch of contractions he counted.

"One." Her body cried for release.

"Two." The anticipation was nearly unbearable.

"Three."

Dana screamed his name as she came. Her orgasm triggered his. Conn went rigid beneath her as he shot his cum at the far reaches of her trembling tissue. He gripped her waist in a bear hug as though he could meld them together. She clung to the ripples of her climax, still flexing her muscles in sets of three as though trained to his will. The euphoria extended longer and longer until it renewed in a second orgasm.

The minutes after her dazzling release passed in a haze. Conn bathed her while whispering his undying love. He lifted her from the tub and dried her, taking care of her every need. Dana still floated in a cloud of sexual completion when he laid her on the bed with unbelievable tenderness.

He climbed under the covers with her then cuddled her against his chest.

"*Mo fiorghra*, there's so much I want to show you." His hands stroked her hair and back. "But only sixty brief minutes remain until the witching hour. What do you want most? Please tell me, what can I give you in the time we have remaining?"

"I want to please you, Conn. Whatever you desire." She placed a soft kiss over his heart.

"Would you be disappointed if I just wanted to lie here and hold you?"

"No. You make me feel safe, peaceful and content. I could lie here with you forever."

For a while they embraced in silence, each thinking their own thoughts.

"I love you, Dana." The sacred vow meant the world to her.

"And I love you, Conn."

"Then you'll grant me a request?" The seriousness of his question didn't escape her. She raised her head to peer into his troubled eyes.

"What do you want?" The despair that met her stare scared her. She guessed what he would ask.

"I can't stay here but I can't go back, Dana. I won't do it." His jaw clenched and his eyes blazed. He looked like a wild animal trapped in a corner. "Give me your gun."

Pain pummeled her chest like a ton of bricks. Horrified, she lied to him for the first time.

"I don't have one."

"Yes, you do. It's in the bedside drawer below the one you keep the dildo in." She had forgotten he'd lived here as long as she had. "I always feared someone would break in and you would pull the fake cock on them by accident."

Despite the gravity of the situation she couldn't stifle a tiny smile. "That probably wouldn't be very effective, huh?"

"I'm serious, Dana. I can't live like that again. I'll take it far away, I won't tell you where, you won't have to see or hear or even know." The conviction in his tone made it clear his mind was made up.

She wrenched from his grasp, appalled. "And what, die somewhere out on the street, alone? No, I won't let you do it. I won't lose you. Besides, did you ever stop to think what that would do to Deirdre? You told me her soul is part of that painting too. What do you think would happen to her if you destroyed yourself and the magic with it?"

"Dana, I don't want an eternity in that haunted painting. It's no life for me." His voice rose in desperation.

"I've been thinking. There may be another solution." At this point, nothing else could be lost. She might as well feel him out on the idea kicking around in her head.

"Go on."

"From what I've gathered so far, these are the restraints. The magic requires a soul. One or two people can enter the painting." At that, his hands tightened involuntarily on her arms. "We both agree I will not become part of the painting but you refuse to return to it. And Deirdre's soul is lost if no one enters the cursed

67

canvas. Does that sound about right?"

Clearly impatient, Conn nodded. "Yes, we know all of that. How does that help?"

"Think like her, Conn. Why doesn't she understand how terrible it was to trap you in there?"

"I guess she believes she granted me some favor. Her vanity makes her believe that being young forever is worth...any price." He bolted upright in bed. "Dear gods, you're a genius. Why didn't I see it before?"

She accepted his quick, fierce kiss before reminding him of reality. "Don't get our hopes up yet. Call her, ask her, and see if it's possible. Find out if she'll do it."

He sobered but nodded. "And if she won't, then I want the gun. If I have to take it from you, I will."

Dana looked at the clock. Eleven thirty-six. "I think it's time. I can feel her. Call her, Conn."

They grasped each other's hands as they knelt together on the bed.

Conn's voice boomed out.

"Deirdre McConalath! Come before me now."

CHAPTER NINE
All Hallow's Day, Eleven thirty-seven p.m.

Conn tensed as the apparition floated through the ceiling. Beside him, Dana shivered. He gathered her closer to his side.

Please, let this work.

"Are you ready to return, Conn?" Both Deirdre's speech and image appeared stronger. The magic had reached its peak.

"We'd like to discuss something with you, Deirdre." Conn desperately wished for Dana's plan to succeed. It made sense. All it had taken was Dana's empathy to devise a solution.

"Time is short, the window is closing. We have to hurry." Deirdre sounded frightened. "Trust me. You do not want to risk the consequences."

"Deirdre, I can't."

The spirit grew angry. Wind shook the bedroom, whipping the curtains from the window and slamming the door. Deirdre grew more substantial and her voice boomed, echoing around the room.

"This is *her* fault. I should never have done this for you. I sacrificed everything for you and you would throw it all away simply because she doesn't love you?" The accusation reverberated as an eerie, shrieking moan, raising the hairs on his neck.

Fearing for Dana's safety, he rose from the bed, tucking her behind him. She leaned close to him, whispering in his ear,

"Don't make her angry. Show her that you appreciate the gift she gave you."

"Deirdre, you don't understand. She does love me." He couldn't stop the smile spreading across his face at the knowledge.

"Then it's settled, you both go. Now." She raised her hands in their direction, a faint blue flame lighting her hands.

"No! Deirdre, you were right earlier. I never understood you. I'm sorry that I didn't look deeper. I appreciate the gift you gave me by preserving me through time to meet Dana. The act was selfless and pure." She calmed at his apology. The curtains stopped flapping and the lights returned to normal.

The flickering image smiled for the first time. Her wrinkled face regained a shred of its former beauty with the gesture.

"What will happen to you if I return to the painting, Deirdre?" Behind him, Dana tensed. He squeezed her hand in reassurance, letting her know he didn't intend to do it.

"My soul is tied to the artwork, I can never move on. I will always linger."

"Deirdre, I want you to take the gift you gave to me. Trade your sentence as an old soul for eternal youth and beauty. Take my place in the painting." He nearly begged her.

She grew brighter and, for a moment, the image of her young self flashed over the visage of the old woman as though she enjoyed the idea of regaining her allure. Even at her strongest, she could not sustain the image of beauty for more than an instant.

"But I love you, Conn. If I do that, you will stay here. You will grow old, wither and eventually die." The creepy voice moaned in sadness.

Dana nudged him aside and spoke to the spirit directly. "Deirdre, please let us give you this in return for bringing us together. Spending this time with each other, though it may seem short to you, is the best gift we could ever imagine. This is all we have to give you in return. Take the chance to recover what you truly loved best."

"Are you certain, Conn?" Deirdre swooped in to examine his expression up close, but the wall behind her began to show through her form.

"Yes, Deirdre. Go quickly, before time runs out. I promise we'll make sure the painting is taken care of. That *you* are taken care of. I can never thank you enough."

The old woman wafted closer to the painting, speeding up as she neared it. The look of elation on her face as she dipped one hand inside alleviated the burden on Conn's conscience. Dana was right, the painting held no suffering for Deirdre.

The woman turned to face them. "Thank you, both of you."

Wild laughter surrounded them, echoing throughout the room when the woman leapt into the painting and struck a playful pose at odds with her haggard appearance. Her body shimmered and rippled. Colors rushed into the gray, lifeless tones of her hair, skin and clothing. Silver strands were painted with black, and the drab dress she wore morphed into the stunning silver gown Conn remembered so well.

Dana gripped his hand so hard he thought she might have broken a bone or two. "Holy shit. No wonder she was upset. She's the most beautiful woman I've ever seen."

He turned her to face him. "Not so. *You're* the most beautiful woman I've ever seen."

Dana shot him reproachful glare. "Don't you ever learn, Conn Hennessey? You'll hurt her feelings."

They studied the painting in time to see the woman wink at Dana. "Make sure you keep a tight rein on him. You were destined for each other."

Before they could respond, the clock on the dresser clicked. It was midnight. A blinding flash obscured their view. When they could see again, the woman stood still, posing seductively with an enticing smile on her gorgeous face.

71

EPILOGUE
All Hallow's Eve, One year later

"Good evening, Deirdre." Dana spoke to the painting as she prepared dinner. "Conn should be home any minute. It's our anniversary, you know. I hope you're enjoying the view in the new apartment. From here you can see the street below and the beautiful sunsets over the skyline. I'll put the radio on again tomorrow, as soon as I unpack it. He told me how much you used to love music."

Just then he came into the room, wrapping his arms around her waist from behind. He kissed her on the check then said, "Hey, Deirdre, how's it going?"

Dana asked, "Is it official?"

He nodded, smiling. "Why don't you tell her the good news?"

"Conn signed the deal with the museum today. We've bequeathed the painting to them on the condition that it always be displayed. You'll have so many admirers; I know you'll be pleased. I picked out the spot myself. There's a lovely view of the gardens and several very handsome paintings on the opposite wall. There's one of a knight and another of a couple dashing pirates."

"And why were you looking so close at those paintings, *fiorghra*?"

Dana wondered if she should continue but she wouldn't ignore her instincts, or the way the hair on the back of her neck had stood up when she passed the artwork.

She pulled Conn around in front of her so she could see both him and Deirdre at once. "Listen, I know this might sound crazy but, then again, who would have believed this…" She gestured at the portrait. "When I walked by that painting of the knight, I felt something."

Conn raised an eyebrow at her. "Something?"

"Yeah, like the something I used to feel when I walked past you."

"You think there's someone in there?" he asked, incredulous.

"I know it. And somehow, I think things are turning out the way they were always meant to be."

Conn scooped her up into his arms, laughing. "*Mo fiorghra*, I don't doubt it for a second." He peeked over his shoulder at the painting. "Excuse us, Deirdre, I need to borrow my wife for a while."

He carried her upstairs to their bedroom, dropping her on the bed. When he climbed in with her, she asked, "So, have we finished everything on your naughty list?" His creativity and imagination had definitely been honed during those nine hundred years of thinking.

"Not even close," he said with a wicked grin.

"Good." Their playful mood turned serious. "I love you, Sir Conn Hennessey."

"I love you too, Dana Hennessey."

REBORN
JAYNE RYLON

CHAPTER ONE
One week ago

"You're sure, Amystia? You're ready?"

My heart soars at the idea. I've craved this for nearly three centuries. "We've only been waiting for Warren to decide for certain. Since he's rejected Sylvia, he's exhausted the list of possible mates. He hasn't shown even a glimmer of interest in another for ages."

I had watched as my mate, King Dagan, bid farewell to the stunning young vampire who'd requested a personal audience. Only millennia of experience in tempering my reactions had prevented me from dancing on my throne when she divulged her news.

Dagan flashes me a radiant grin, broad enough to permit a glimpse of his razor-sharp canines. The unmitigated joy radiating from him thrills me to the core. He crushes me in his arms then whirls us both around. We spin ten feet off the parquet floor of the royal chambers. My ornate dress fans out behind us. For once I am glad of the formal attire I'm forced to wear to match my station as Queen of the United Vampiric Covens. The beaded lace bodice and flowing silk train seem fitting for the proposal we're about to make. Not to mention the military cut jacket, embroidered with the symbols of his ultimate rank, which hugs Dagan's impressive build.

"I don't want to wait another moment." I rest my forehead on

Dagan's brow while I stroke his smooth cheek. The intensity of his maroon eyes still has the power to shock me. Especially when he's as aroused as he is now.

"We've waited long enough. Where is he?" Dagan trails his lips along the pulse hammering in my throat as I close my eyes then search the castle for the other half of my heart. I'm always able to sense his presence.

"The laboratory. He seems... agitated."

Dagan smoothes the furrow of my brow then scoops me into his arms. "No need to worry, love. He's probably just frustrated over dismissing another very willing companion. You know how it disturbs him to injure anyone's pride. Shall we cheer him up?"

"Let's."

I squeeze my eyes closed as my mate flies along the corridors to Warren's tower. I never have gotten used to the way the two of them zip from point to point instead of gliding at a more sedate pace. As we near, a series of crashes reverberates through the stone foundations of the castle.

"Dagan..." An ominous frisson of warning tugs at my nerves. "Perhaps we should come back later. He's not responding to my calls."

Though all vampires have paranormal talents, mine have always been strongest when sensing and communicating with loved ones, even from great distances. Just a few hundred yards away now, and closing rapidly as we climb the spiral staircase, I should be able to hold a conversation with Warren. Yet I cannot dent the vampire sorcerer's concentration on his task.

"I won't waste even one more hour, Amystia. He'll have to resume his experiment tomorrow. Or maybe next week, after we've finished celebrating." Dagan barges through the oak plank door without so much as knocking.

The soaring bookcases that line every inch of the curved walls of Warren's sanctuary come into view as I blink open my eyes. Then a streak of black whizzes toward my face. Before I can react, Dagan twists to the side and drops me. Whatever was flying at me slams into the left half of my mate's chest with enough impact to launch him into the air over my head.

I stare, horrified, as he catapults through a row of beakers and other assorted glassware on the table nearby before destroying four entire shelves of ancient tomes with his limp body. Why didn't he slow himself?

"Dagan!" I rush to his side only to find him unconscious, something I've never seen in all our years together. Not even when he'd been ambushed by forty young rebels, or after he'd been hit by a tank, had he wavered before his injuries healed over seconds later. But now he lies crumpled on the stonework.

I pivot, searching for Warren. He's standing across the open space, his hand outstretched toward the line of targets he'd been aiming at before we intruded. Abject terror freezes his expression.

"Help him," I shout. "Warren!"

A blur streaks toward me. Then he is there, kneeling at my side.

"What have I done?" he wails as he drags Dagan from the rubble. "Dagan. Please wake up. Please."

Buttons pop off the fancy coat I had so recently admired. The dusty, ripped fabric is cast aside as Warren searches for the injury that has felled the mightiest vampire in recorded history.

I cradle Dagan's ultra-pale face while Warren examines my mate. My voice will not work as I wish. Instead, I reach out with my mind.

Wake up, Dagan. You're frightening Warren.

Amystia.

Relief dissolves the alarm flooding me when he responds, though the slight waver in his tone concerns me.

Are you all right, love? That... evil... headed straight for you. What the hell was that?

I'm fine, Dag. You have to come back now. Ask Warren yourself.

A ragged groan accompanies the flicker of his eyes opening. The sheen of lust that had brightened them has vanished but he'll recover within minutes. As he has done every other time he's sustained critical injuries in battle.

"Dagan!" Warren grasps his shoulders then props him against a cabinet.

"What exactly are you researching up here, Advisor? And when can we equip the guards with that spell?"

I grin at the attempted humor though Warren only stares in

shock.

"It's not something to joke of. I shouldn't have attempted it on-site. Reckless! At least I didn't perform the incantation correctly." He rakes his fine-boned fingers through his mussed hair as he mumbles to himself, a habit I adore.

"What are you saying? I'd be tempted to believe I hit my head harder than I thought but you never make sense when you rant about your studies." Dagan rubs one hand over his torso. The motion draws my attention to his sculpted form and the charred starburst covering his abdomen. That certainly hadn't been there this morning.

"It's something that could keep us from war forever. The ultimate weapon, devised by the ancients. I thought I'd patched together the proper spell several weeks ago. But I had shelved further trials. They're too risky." A grimace mars his youthful visage. "Forgive me, Dagan. Today I required a distraction…"

"We heard about Sylvia." I bridge the gap between the men. One hand cups Dagan's jaw while the other rests on Warren's shoulder. Their fingers rise to mine, curling over my hands.

"I couldn't accept her. It wasn't fair to promise her something I don't have to give. My heart is not my own."

I want to ease the dejection in his eyes.

Don't reveal our plans, Amystia. Not like this. Let's wait until tonight. I'll be recovered by then. We'll make it special for us all. He deserves that.

Warren's gaze flickers to the ugly mark, which still isn't fading. "Are you certain you're not suffering? The spell is intended to be lethal to our kind. Resistant to all cures, even magic."

"It burns, though not much. I'm positive it will be a distant memory by dinner."

But it wasn't.

CHAPTER TWO
Three days later

I cling to the ladder as I knock an inch of dust from the antique volumes ringing the top levels of Warren's laboratory. I refuse to glance down. I've never mastered levitating myself. The cure has to be here. It's my final hope. We've already searched through every other tome in the palace. Vague references, veiled allusions and fragmented instructions are the best we've uncovered.

"Amystia, be careful!" Dagan's concerned bellow sounds hollow to me. Tingles run along my spine as he reaches out with his power. A few days ago, it would have supported me as sure as an iron fist but now I'm certain I would fall straight through the weak likeness of his former ability and plummet to the stone below if I let go. Though I'd heal soon enough, there is not a moment to spare.

Warren's essence mixes with Dagan's as he lassoes both the books and me, then controls our descent to the floor. How can I not care for a man who protects my mate's ego?

Dagan's brow is dotted with sweat but satisfaction tugs one corner of his mouth into a somber grin. "Perhaps the sickness is not as bad as it seems."

How I wish that were true.

"You should be in bed, resting." Warren joins us by the entryway where Dagan leans propped against the doorframe.

"I have things to attend to, things that need to be addressed. Until they are resolved, my mind cannot settle." He scrubs his palm over his jaw.

Warren loops his arm around Dagan's shoulder. The gesture would seem friendly if I didn't realize how much of Dagan's weight he supports as he guides my mate to his private chambers. I curl up on the rich brocade covering Warren's bed. Dagan joins me, sitting with his shoulders against the headboard.

I rest my head in his lap, biting my lip to keep from sobbing. Warren lounges on the other side of Dagan's trim hips.

"What's bothering you, my friend?" Warren falls into the familiar routine. As Dagan's key advisor, he often acts as a sounding board.

"It's clear that unless we uncover a miracle, I am going to die."

I gasp. We have avoided the truth for three days. Hearing the blunt declaration rips my heart in two. How can I bear to live without him?

"Do not give up hope yet. We have found references to a ritual that could reverse the effects of the spell." Warren's confidence bolsters my hope but when I peer into his face, I see the tears in his eyes. He does not believe.

"A fool's errand, friend. Attempting such magic on the rumor of legend is folly. You would only destroy yourself. That cannot be allowed. When I am gone, you must look after Amystia."

The intensity of Dagan's determination would frighten even the most badass vamp but Warren merely nods.

"You still trust me?" His coarse whisper cannot contain the boundless agony I sense in him.

"We adore you, Warren. Our people rely on you. They will need you."

He abandons the bed, pacing the room. "They should destroy me for what I have done!"

"Come here." The order from his king is undeniable.

Warren sinks onto the mattress once more.

"You have been our closest friend, and sometimes lover, for nearly a thousand years. Do you not yet realize the respect I have for you? I instructed the council that, should I fall, Amystia will rule with you by her side. They could hope for no better leaders.

That is not my concern." Dagan's hand wanders over the shocked features of Warren's face. "Do not make me leave this world with even a sliver of doubt. Prove to me that you will not let my mate suffer for your guilt. You must take her, hold her, shelter her. Always."

"I swear to you that I will." With his gaze still averted, Warren grips Dagan's wrist with enough force that my mate winces. He is worsening by the minute.

"Show me that you can still love her though you no longer look me in the eye."

My jaw goes slack as I realize Dagan's intent. "You're ill!"

"I'm not so sick that I can't savor the most glorious thing on earth. I want to share you one last time." The pure devotion in his eyes makes arguing impossible.

Warren groans beside me. "It's difficult to be gentle when everything inside me rages against injustice. I won't touch her without control."

"I cannot rest until you do. Grant me this peace of mind."

Dagan strokes my hair where it drapes over his thigh. I would do anything to soothe him, either of them. Warren's pain affects me too. As usual, our king is right. We must take this chance to love together one final time or Warren will never recover. I cannot lose them both.

I shift on the bed, lying on my back between Dagan's spread legs, my head propped on his chest. His thick arousal nudges my spine. Untying the laces that cross the front of my long robe, he spreads the fabric wide in the wake of his hands. A cool breeze fans across my bare breasts and the slick flesh between my thighs. Memories assault me, making my pussy weep for all the pleasure Dagan and Warren have given me through the ages.

"Ah yes, you smell delicious, love. Intoxicating."

I should feel some dose of remorse that, even as my mate deteriorates, I hunger for both him and the man we had intended to bond as our permanent third. Instead, all I can do is surrender to the instincts that urge me to accept their touch.

Dagan cups my neck in his hand, sending shivers along the length of my spine as I recall the times he has drained his fill from me. The fingers of his other hand swirl over my collarbones, between my breasts then along my arm, making me squirm with the need for more.

"Get drunk on her, Warren."

Our lover shoots me an uncertain glance. I widen the vee of my thighs, inviting him to sample the arousal he has inspired. Faster than I can detect, he flies from his perch on the edge of the bed. His tongue swipes along the cleft of my sex, gathering the dew from my lips.

"Yes, take more of her."

Warren moans as he buries his face in my pussy, devouring my sopping flesh with desperate laps. He flicks his talented tongue around my opening, dipping inside just enough to tease before tracing the valley of my labia to my clit. When his lips envelop the bundle of nerves, the pleasure threatens to drown me.

I arch into Dagan's hold. The position tilts my head back until Dagan's mouth descends on mine. He claims me with a fierce kiss that shows me just how much he enjoys watching our lover consume me.

He cups my breasts, kneading the globes. My nipples stab his palms. Familiar lust overtakes my senses. I abandon all thought and embrace sensation.

My knees press closer to my torso when Warren spreads his fingers beneath my knees, pushing them up and apart. The pressure lifts my rear from the duvet, clearing a path for Warren to extend his laving to Dagan's tight balls. The six-pack abs of my mate flex against my spine, making his cock jerk between us.

"Overachiever." Dagan growls against my lips.

Our lover's wicked tongue lashes us both. The pulsing aura of the men's passion surrounds me, enhancing my own pleasure. I writhe in their grasp. The motion grinds my ass against Dagan's cock. I wish I could tip forward enough to take him inside me but he subdues my struggles with the band of his muscular arms around my waist.

"No, love," he whispers. "I want Warren to take you. I need to know he still can."

The younger vampire lifts his head from where he'd been working my clit with soft pulls of his full lips even as he caressed Dagan's wrinkled sac. I whimper in frustration. Despite the inferno burning inside my belly, I am still frightened, empty.

I need to be possessed—reassured that I will not suffer alone, as self-centered as that may be.

I squirm from between my lovers then turn onto my hands and knees to present myself to Warren. His fingers tremble as they curl around my hips. Yet he makes no move to enter me. He has always been eager before.

My lips nuzzle the engorged shaft of Dagan's hard-on. If one of them does not take me soon I will impale myself on their flesh. My breasts are heavy as they hang beneath me, my restless motion dragging my nipples over the intricate embroidery of the coverlet.

Warren teases my flanks with featherlight strokes of his fingertips. Still, he hesitates.

"She needs *you*, Dagan. I'm a pale imitation. The bastard who has stolen her king. I don't deserve a reward for that."

"She *deserves* a mate. One who loves her as you do. Take what she's offering. Don't hurt her further."

I realize I'm crying only when Dagan dashes the tears from my cheeks. He licks the liquid from his hand. The tingle of his power washes over me. He reaches for Warren. The energy is no longer enough to force compliance but it still clarifies his demand. It wraps around the base of Warren's solid erection then tugs him toward my waiting pussy.

The head of his cock bumps my sensitive opening, causing me to whimper. I rock into the contact, gaining the barest hint of penetration.

"Amy," he groans. "Are you sure?"

"I need you, Warren. Please, join with me."

We cry out together when his stiff flesh skewers me with one long thrust. He collapses, blanketing my back as he begins to move inside me. The even glide of his hips fills me to capacity on every stroke. I clench around him, struggling to keep him buried to the hilt.

In this position, his balls tap my clit on every pass, driving me wild. I open my mouth on a moan. My lips bump into Dagan's steel-hard cock. My eyes flutter open. A bead of pre-cum rolls down the flared purple head of his shaft. I reach out my tongue to lick it away.

Dagan's broad hand fists in my hair, for the first time ever preventing me from tasting him. I never thought I'd see the day when he refused a blowjob.

"Could this harm her?" Dagan glances at Warren, whose face hovers inches from mine. The heat of his labored breathing bathes my cheek.

"No, the taint resides in your blood alone. As long as she doesn't drink from your veins she will remain unaffected."

Dagan's other hand tangles in Warren's hair. With slight pressure on the back of our heads, he guides each of us to one side of his erection. I meet Warren's gaze around the throbbing shaft. Though he continues to fuck me with that devastating rhythm, I can see we both long for more. Together, we reach out our tongues and lick a synchronized line along the entire length of Dagan's cock.

My mate roars as we continue to flick, suck and nip his painfully aroused hard-on. Warren begins to take me harder, his hips slapping my ass. The motion forces me to dip lower, so I open my lips wide to mouth Dagan's balls. They shift against my tongue, drawing closer to his core.

With more room to maneuver, Warren engulfs the tip then slides down Dagan's pole until our lips meet in a heated kiss.

"After five thousand years...you'd think it impossible to surprise me." Dagan's fingers knot in my hair, keeping me in place though I make no attempt to retreat.

Who would willingly abandon this rapture?

Warren, who tends to seek an edge of pain with his pleasure, moans. The vibration shakes Dagan's balls and my lips around them. Our lover pumps into my sopping pussy, igniting flame after flame of ecstasy inside me. The increased pace of his strokes heightens the intensity of his balls slapping my clit.

I let Dagan slip from my lips, afraid that I might lose control and bite him in my mindless passion.

"Yes, Warren. Fuck her well. I bet she's clamping around your cock now." A sheen of sweat glistens on Dagan's abdomen. His fingers twist in the sheets beneath him.

As much as the sight arouses him, I will never be able to outlast him. Warren's shaft stretches my clinging sheath with every penetration. The ridge of his cock head and the prominent veins caress me from the inside. The sight of him devouring my mate fuels my desire. But Dagan knows how to push me over the edge.

"Her sweet pussy loves your cock. Pull out, Warren."

He groans in protest but does as commanded after several more full thrusts.

"Tease her, make her beg for it."

The tip of his cock returns, blazing hot on my skin. He taps the blunt head against my clit, never pausing the pattern of his sucking. I watch his cheeks hollow around Dagan's shaft a moment before my muscles begin to spasm.

"Please, Warren, fill me. I don't want to come without you. Please! I need you!"

I groan in defeat when the first ripple of my abdomen signals my impending orgasm.

"Now. Fuck her, Warren."

Stars zoom past my eyes as the world explodes. Warren's thick erection parts the swollen flesh of my pussy. He slams inside me, riding me hard, taking me higher. The fierce grasp of my undulating tissue drags him with me into climax. His throat flexes around his shout and Dagan's cock before he too pulls off the magnificent erection.

Warren pulses inside me, flooding my pussy with stream after stream of his passion.

At the sight of our release, my mate joins us though no one is touching his cock. It twitches against his abdomen then sprays a fountain of cum in arc after arc. One pearly strand drapes across my face. Warren reaches out to lick it from my cheek, inciting another batch of thrusts and grunts that I match with an equal number of contractions.

I catch several droplets on my tongue then savor the taste with a satisfied hum.

Warren continues to shuttle inside me long after we are spent. He moves softly until his wilting cock slips from my hold. We groan together then help Dagan rest against the pillows.

We take up our posts, one on each side of my mate. My head rests on his chest, allowing me to witness the knowing exchange between the two men.

"Thank you, Warren." Dagan draws our lover to him for an extended kiss then cradles us both against his weakening body.

"You two will do just fine without me."

CHAPTER THREE
Today

I am a selfish creature.

Five thousand years of wild nights with my soulmate haven't quenched my thirst for his love or slaked my hunger for his touch. But as the vitality leaks from Dagan's crimson irises in a wash of bloody tears, I know there's only time for one more tryst. And one more fight. I cannot let him go without them.

Friends, nobles and staff file from the room after saying somber goodbyes. Warren lingers longest before bestowing a final, enduring kiss on pale lips. Pain obscures my vision. It prevents me from realizing we're alone until I hear Dagan's whispered entreaty.

"Lay with me, *Amystia*." Beloved light. He imparted the term of endearment, popular in his youth, on me before the pyramids. The pure label predated the modern concepts of good and evil that draw false boundaries on an endlessly complex universe.

Dagan's raspy voice is only a faint shadow of the resounding timbre he possessed less than a week ago. Seven days—a blink compared to millennia of existence. How well I know, each moment is precious. A single millisecond, a slip of the hand and a whim of fate can steal every modicum of bliss from one's existence.

Who would have believed an accident could claim the life of the world's oldest and most powerful vampire when endless assassins could not?

I lower myself to the satin sheets that cradle his withering body. Unbidden, my finger traces the ominous black line leading from the wound, along his veins, ending less than an inch from his still heart. The damage has progressed so much closer in the past hour.

It won't be long now.

"Come." Dagan spreads his arms wide. The strain around his mouth at the simple gesture is more than I can bear. I'm afraid to lay my head on his now frail shoulder, in the spot I've found solace and shelter for all my long life.

The corner of his wicked mouth slants up in a ghost of a smile. "You could never hurt me, Amystia. Come."

"I need you." Guilt infuses my gut for my weakness. I should be the one to comfort him, and yet I find myself clinging to his chilled torso, terrified to let go. My shaking body rattles against his as my control slips. "I'm begging you, as I have never done in all our time together. Let me perform the ritual."

"No. It's only a myth. I will not allow you to risk yourself, or Warren." My plea upsets Dagan. He struggles to draw breath. Though it pains me to see, I take the opportunity to argue my case when it would otherwise be impossible to get a word past my stubborn and dominant mate.

"I cannot live without you."

He coughs. The alien sound of suffering from a creature immune to sickness terrifies me. I send a thin stream of power to soothe his labored gasps as I stroke midnight locks from his handsome face.

"Grief has never destroyed a vampire. Especially not one as strong as you, Queen."

"I'll be the first, remembered in some tragic song, infamous among the covens. Is that what you want?" I'm not really kidding, though I try to sound as though I am. "If I cannot keep you here, I will follow where you go."

"You've always had a flair for the dramatic." Love radiates from his attempted grin in waves and he draws strength from our bond. "But this time, I will not change my mind. Your soul is priceless. More valuable to me than anything else. Including my own."

"But…"

"Amystia," The thread of sound frayed, near to snapping. "It's too late. Do not waste our time. Let me hold you."

It is impossible to deny a dying man his final wish. I snuggle into his welcoming arms, our bodies forming a single unit, and lift my head to brush my lips against his as I have infinite times before. Desperation, longing and fear drive my frantic kiss. As always, Dagan becomes a sturdy receptacle for my turmoil of emotions—collecting them, bottling them and grounding me.

When I surface to gaze into his eyes, he whispers against my mouth, "I'm sorry I can't love you one last time."

With a thought, I banish our clothes to the bedroom floor. I nuzzle the sweet spot at the base of his neck, then lick my way down his muscular chest to scrape my fang across his nipple, just as he likes best. "You can."

Before he can argue, I slide my palm lower, past the delectable ridges of his steel-hard abs, to cup his flaccid penis. Muted hunger flares in his eyes. Even on his deathbed, Dagan wants me nearly as much as I want him. As I have done during the deepest hours of previous nights, when our lust outlasted the capability of his body, I use my power to direct the flow of his hot, delicious blood. His cock inflates below my hand, transforming into the thick shaft that fills me to perfection.

If only it were so easy to stop the progression of his poison.

The weight of my full breasts rests on his muscular arm and my crimson fingernail traces the prominent vein that decorates the underside of his cock while memories of thousands of shared ecstasies bombard my mind.

"Hurry, Amystia." The pleading in his voice stems from more than desire. If it had been that alone, I could have teased him for days. And oftentimes had.

I wrap currents of air around myself until I float into position, straddling his lean hips. Though our lovemaking is rushed, I'm wet and ready to hold Dagan as close as I can. Primal instincts take control. I hover over the blunt tip of his impressive erection before sinking onto it bit by bit.

It feels like coming home.

The intensity of our situation enhances the familiar sensation of our bodies gliding against each other but worry prevents me from soaking in the pleasure of our union. For Dagan, I work my magic and all my charms to raise him higher. I stroke his chest with my palms, lick a glistening trail over the seam of his lips and replace his suffering with desire.

Using more tricks, I enchant the satin sheet he lies on to caress every inch of his fevered skin while I ride his full erection. Beads of sweat dot Dagan's brow. I clasp his hands in mine against the bed as I prepare to grant him one final release. I focus my energy into an ethereal hand and use it to draw swirling spirals of delight across the sensitive sac housing his balls.

Words are beyond us now but the pleasure is plain to read in my lover's eyes. Our spirits twine together so tight, I can hear his thoughts as though they are my own. My brave, honorable mate struggles to resist until I am ready to find satisfaction with him.

I don't think it will be possible this time.

I'm amazed when, with one last burst of strength, he summons his power to flutter against my clit in the single motion guaranteed to throw me into oblivion. I shatter around him, the spasms of my flesh dragging him with me. Ecstasy permeates our bodies, our souls, and the power of our joining crackles through the very air around us.

A satisfied smile registers on Dagan's face. His eyes open wide as his gaze locks onto mine. He mouths, "I love you."

Then, he is gone.

I reach out to him with my mind.

Nothing exists.

CHAPTER FOUR

Disbelief swamps my senses but even that cannot eclipse the agony shredding my insides. For a moment, I observe the lifeless shell of my mate before overcoming my instinctive distaste and sinking my fangs into the thick artery at the base of his neck. I have not lived this long, and served as Queen of our people, without learning to do what I must despite my personal feelings.

Dagan's blood is bitter. Rancid poison and the stench of death ruin the sacred flavor of my mate. I ignore nature's warning, swallowing despite the reflexive reaction of my body, which urges me to purge the spoiled food.

There isn't a moment to waste. Even as I drain the last bit of lethal toxin from Dagan, I call out. My dignified status doesn't generally lend itself to shrieking, but my royal bearing can't conceal the horror in my heart.

"Warren!"

The bedroom door slams open and the tall, lithe vampire appears at my side with preternatural speed. His gorgeous face crumples in sorrow as he absorbs the scene before him. Dagan's wasted body, the fresh puncture wound on his neck and the drip of still-warm blood from my fangs declare my intent.

"What have you done, Amy? There's no going back now. You have to attempt the Phoenix Incantation." It isn't a question. Warren's low voice covers a core of steel. The perfect complements to Dagan's brawn and savvy, his rational mind and

93

dedication to academics have earned him the title of King Dagan's most trusted advisor. But it is his quiet confidence, proven loyalty and underlying vulnerability that have made him our closest friend for a thousand years.

During the past week, Warren and I had frantically searched the tomes of the compound's extensive library for a cure but all we uncovered were cryptic references to an arcane rite.

The Phoenix Incantation.

"I'm sorry, Warren." He lifts me from the bed. I take the solace offered in his steady embrace with unabashed greed, speaking in hushed tones against the warm plane of his chest as he holds me. "I didn't want you to be torn between your king's command and my insistence. This way, either the poison or the magic will reunite me with Dagan. I can't bear to be separated from him."

"Did he give you his blood willingly?" Over my head, Warren's tear-filled stare fixes on the remains of the man we both loved most. My skin tingles as he levitates the corpse to the waiting marble platform. The whisper of satin declares the black sheet has become a shroud.

I shake my head in sadness, "He forbade me to try. I took it right after…"

"That will make things more difficult. The incantation works best when the subject seeds their life force with the will to be anchored to the mortal world." Warren voices his concerns aloud. It's endearing. We'd been over this plan many times in the past days, after all optimism for Dagan's recovery had evaporated.

"You still plan to execute the magic alone?" The flash of hurt in Warren's eyes adds another weight to the burden on my soul.

"Yes. Direct me. There's only an hour or so until dawn." The complex summons would take time to prepare. In all the obscure references, we'd found only one consistent instruction. The ritual had to be complete before daybreak following the death of a soulmate.

"What will you use to draw his essence to you? The magic requires something strong enough to pierce through the underworld."

"Memories. I know it didn't work for the ancients, Warren.

But Dagan and I shared millennia of experience—far more than the average lifespan during the dark times."

Warren shakes his head in vehement denial. "I've been thinking. There's a better way."

"Does it place you at risk?" I can't bear to have his death on my conscience.

"I would forsake my life for either of you as my king and queen and my soul for your friendship." He strokes a stray tress of hair from my face with unrivaled tenderness. Warren has always embodied a softness Dagan lacks. His refusal to answer my question gives me all the information I need.

"In case things don't go as planned…" I can't bring myself to voice the worst. "Our people will look to you for guidance, for leadership. They need you, Warren."

"And what of my needs?" His graceful, long-fingered hands cup my face, tilting it toward his. "I don't wish to be sentenced to a life alone. You should understand that."

The sincerity in his gray eyes tugs at my heart but I won't condemn him to a fate worse than death. Failure in the Phoenix Incantation results in the voiding of the conjurer's soul.

"You belong here, Warren. You're barely twelve hundred years old. You have your whole life ahead of you. In time, you'll find your true mate and forget about us." I bestow a serene kiss on his lush mouth to ease the sting of my rejection.

"No one could ever replace you in my heart." He pushes me away then spins to face the shrouded form across the room, his fists clenched at his sides. An uncharacteristic crack in his reserve allows his anger and frustration to pour out. "It's my fucking fault he's dead!"

I reach up and lay my hand on his shoulder. His violent trembling vibrates down my outstretched arm. "It was an accident. No one blames you. Dagan knew better than to enter your laboratory without knocking."

Warren faces me. The unveiled misery in his expression knocks me back several steps. "I'll never forgive myself if I don't try everything within my power to bring him home."

The ultimate truth of his statement rings between us. Who am I to destroy his chance for absolution? "What are you suggesting?"

"I've seen the power of your love for each other during sex."
He hesitates as though gathering courage to propose the most
logical solution. I already know what he'll say. As usual, he's
right. "Together, we'll call him to us with passion."

"You read the warnings, Warren. The magic will ensnare any
participants in the rite." The ramifications of his scheme swim in
my mind. "This would bind you to us forever."

"You wouldn't want to have me? Or is it Dagan who would
object?" Uncertainty colors his automatic response. How have I
missed the depth of his emotions? His cool, bookish façade hides
feelings that run deeper than I imagined.

I gather his stiff body to mine and squeeze him before
meeting his searching gaze. "Dagan and I have often talked of
proposing a more permanent relationship between us. We only
delayed because we wanted to be sure you had the chance to
search for a lover who could be yours alone. In fact, that's why
we came to you that day. Once you'd dismissed Sylvia, we knew
you were meant to be ours."

He blinks back the tears gracing his full lashes like dew on a
crisp morning. "The two of you are all I've ever wanted. The
others were just a distraction. And now I stand to lose you both.
Let me do this."

Warren's fingers dig into my upper arms with bruising
pressure, a testament to his desperation. He has never touched
me with anything but the utmost care before.

"How do we begin?" I ask. Relief erodes the tension in his
pinched expression. His head dips forward until his forehead
rests on mine and we stand eye to eye for a long moment. Then
the scholar returns and he's all business.

"Stay here."

Warren uses his gift for preternatural speed to run to his
laboratory and gather supplies. He transports a sturdy table made
of scarred planks along with all the necessary supplies in the
blink of an eye. He wastes no time, levitating me onto the rough
wood. The coarse surface abrades my bare skin. I shift restlessly,
in search of a comfortable position. Before I find one, his power
wraps around my wrists and ankles, tugging them to the corners
of the platform.

I gape at Warren from my vulnerable, spread-eagle pose.

Where is the careful, submissive man I've come to love?

"There is no time to waste on pleasantries, Queen. Dawn approaches."

The menacing snick of metal shackles encircling my limbs both frightens and thrills me. Instinct prods me to test the binding but the mystical artifacts prevent my magic from undoing the clasps. I am truly held at Warren's mercy.

Before my eyes, a silver ceremonial robe replaces his modern clothing, transforming his innocent appearance into the image of a powerful sorcerer straight out of legend. If anyone can save Dagan, this man can. I swallow past the lump in my throat when he turns to a thick, leather-bound book—the one he compiles his notes in—lying open on a stand nearby. Sandy hair feathers over Warren's forehead in familiar disarray as he peruses the flowing script.

He mutters to himself as he reads. "Yes, third circle here. Then the forms, finally the call." He nods one last time before assessing me. His intense stare burns my bound body. "Dagan's spirit won't be able to resist you."

Warren raises his hands, palms up. His eyes close and all the lights douse. Panic threatens to overwhelm me as I struggle to see in the supernatural darkness. Night never blinds a vampire. I thrash against the restraints, terrified, but I can't break free.

"Warren?" I hardly recognize the feeble croak that escapes my throat.

His fine-boned hand clamps over my mouth an instant before he whispers in my ear. The murmur comes so soft I wouldn't be able to hear him if not for my augmented senses. "The incantation has begun. Any misspoken words can have unintended consequences. You must not use your powers either, they can interfere. Forgive me, Queen."

I wonder what he's apologizing for a moment before a scrap of cloth wads in my mouth, trapped by another strip bound behind my head. Warren's hand lingers, stroking my hair until I can control my instinct to fight. Once more, his barely audible voice snakes through my fear. "Last chance to stop, after this we're committed or the results will be disastrous. Are you sure?"

I nod, the only way I can communicate. Nothing can revoke my determination to attempt the ritual if there's even a remote chance of success. Besides, the poison I ingested already burns through my veins. The successful spell presents my single chance at survival.

Once again, Warren removes his support to continue the rite. I'm alone in the dark.

Is this what it's like when you die?

My skin crawls, my nipples draw tight and goose bumps rise up on my arms as powerful sorcery pervades the room. One by one, red candles illuminate the inky blackness as Warren chants in a monotonous tone. The flickering light outlines his sleek shape as he circles my immobilized form. With every flame that ignites, an answering spike of arousal slams through my core. There is something seductive about the authority he wields and my helplessness before him. He imbues my body with the desire to attract Dagan's soul.

The rhythm of his mellifluous speech entrances me. Several minutes pass, maybe as long as a half hour, before I'm aware of him standing beside my shoulder. Hundreds of candles, positioned in three rings encircling me, set the room ablaze.

My eyes widen as Warren plucks one from the iron stand and then holds it aloft over my exposed torso. His gaze flicks to mine as his hand tilts, causing the molten wax to bulge along the lip of the candle. The power surging in the air swirls the curls around Warren's face. Beautiful and dangerous, he towers over me.

The first drop of maroon paraffin falls as though in slow motion. Warren's arm lifts high, providing the material plenty of time to cool. I watch with a mix of fascination and horror as the scalding blob races ever nearer. I'm thankful for the fabric that muffles my moan of pain, and arousal, when the bead finally splatters across the taut skin of my abdomen.

Something wild rears up in Warren's stare. Then he releases a thin stream of wax that forms the foundational line of a spell form down the center of my torso. I writhe within the confines of my bonds, the heat soaking into my core and setting me on fire. Moisture gathers between my legs while Warren continues unaffected. All the while, he maintains the ancient language of the incantation.

I brace myself when the next spurt of liquid drapes across my breasts. My heels drum on the wood beneath me but the sting quickly morphs into desire. Three, four more times, Warren decorates my flesh with the scorching substance. Each flare of pain mixes with the enchantment pulsing around us, instilling me with uncontrollable lust. I would beg him to touch me if this damn gag didn't dampen my cries.

He returns the candle, now a sliver of its previous size, to the ceremonial holder. His hands fan out over my abdomen and his voice raises. The invocation reaches a fevered pitch.

Then all is silent.

The atmosphere is heavy, laden with energy. Warren unties the knot on my gag then grabs a goblet from a pedestal near the tome of instructions. He gulps—his masculine throat bobbing—before leaning over me, removing the cloth from my mouth then sealing his lips over mine. The acidic tang of ceremonial wine spills onto my tongue as he shares the offering.

Hungry, I delve into the recesses of his sweet mouth to sop up the last drops. He kisses me with unleashed fervor the like of which I've never experienced from our docile playmate. His robe vanishes then he flies on top of me, steamy flesh pressed to steamy flesh. My head drops with a *thunk* against the table, exposing my neck to Warren in the clearest sign of a vampire's trust and desire.

I imagine Dagan. How he would love to watch Warren ravish me while I sucked Dagan's glorious cock! A faint pressure daubs my lips as though I can actually feel his engorged tip applying for entrance.

Warren distracts me from the sensation as he nibbles his way between my breasts, his long body nestled in the cradle of my thighs. His tongue laves my belly, soothing the sting of his love bites. He's always been attentive to my pleasure.

I moan when he suckles one hard nipple against his razor sharp teeth for a moment before continuing his journey, leaving a trail of passion in his wake. His elegant hands surround my hips, gripping them tight before he buries his face in my pussy.

Warren's wicked tongue tortures me, flicking and flittering in delicious eddies around my clit and the swells of my engorged labia. I strain against the shackles, desperate to press my wet folds against his talented mouth. A whimper of delicious frustration seeps from my parted lips.

Being bound always enhances my desire. It reminds me of the time Dagan captured my wrists then pinned me to our oversized bed, giving Warren free rein to take pleasure from my exposed flesh. Instead, he'd made a study of all the ways to tease me, driving me wild—just as he was now—for hours until I nearly collapsed from exhaustion after dozens of orgasms. My forearms prickle in the spot Dagan's hands had encircled.

A ray of panic invades my sphere of longing. What if we cannot reach my mate? The light touch on my arm evaporates as my focus scatters. Warren's head snaps up, his silent communication imploring me to concentrate.

He provides incentive, his finger dipping inside the moist entrance of my pussy. Another traces the tight ring of muscle below. The dual sensations force me to recall the special times I've spent sandwiched between the sweat-slicked bodies of my two lovers.

Dagan has always been an ass man. He loves to fondle, spank and fuck my rear. While I relish submitting to my mate in the most primitive display of possession, being with both Dagan and Warren enhances the experience. It allows my mate to take what he needs yet provides me the means to find my own satisfaction. Nothing can compare to the sensation of two hard cocks pistoning inside me while I'm cocooned in the heat from Dagan's muscular body and Warren's trim form.

Warren's exploratory digits seem to expand inside me. I can no longer deny that there's more at work than our earthly flesh. I tense then peek at the vampire between my legs. His concerned gaze fixes on mine, careful to observe the situation. He nods, reassuring me and driving me higher when his face nuzzles my pussy.

I gasp when he sucks my clit into his warm, moist mouth. Pleasure zings through my veins, forcing me to rock my hips, begging for more. I watch him ingest every drop of my arousal so I witness the moment when his control snaps. His eyes turn wild, almost possessed. He lunges up then covers my body.

With one thrust, Warren enters me completely. The sudden intrusion of his long cock shocks my accommodating muscles. I can only remember one other time he conquered me with an intensity nearing this. Dagan had commanded Warren to ride me hard while my mate watched, stroking his thick erection. All the while he had coached Warren, encouraging him to fuck me harder, faster. Just as Warren is doing now.

On the edge of my vision, an insubstantial apparition coalesces. I can almost picture Dagan as he was that night, fist wrapped around his meaty cock, his chest bellowing with harsh breaths as he witnessed Warren use me and make me love it.

Warren's shaft jerks inside me and, somehow, I know he is remembering the same liaison. His thrusts grow frenzied. His steel-hard flesh rasps against a delicious spot deep inside me. On any other night, it would be more than enough to make me come.

My orgasm is elusive. After so many lifetimes with Dagan, I struggle to tip over the edge in his absence. No matter how skilled Warren is, or how amazing his long cock feels stroking my pussy, I miss my connection with Dagan.

I conjure an image of the most erotic night of our lives. The night Dagan and I first discussed mating Warren.

After several rounds of escalating lovemaking, Warren had buried himself inside me one last time while Dagan recovered his stamina. I took Dagan's half-hard cock in my mouth, simply enjoying the taste of our mingled essence and the heavy weight of his shaft on my tongue. I tried to fondle his balls with one hand but our positions limited the motion of my arm.

I rolled away, letting him slip from my lips, intending to pleasure his sac with my mouth. Before I could, Warren captured my jaw and guided me to him for a searing kiss. His moan, and the thickening of his shaft inside me, made it clear he enjoyed the flavor of Dagan's musk. We turned together, me to lave Dagan's testicles and Warren to steal his first taste of cock.

Warren never faltered in his pounding rhythm inside me as he engulfed Dagan's instantly rejuvenated erection in wet heat. From my vantage point, I watched Warren's throat flex as he worked the head of Dagan's cock while I lapped at my mate's balls. When Dagan fisted his hand in Warren's hair then tugged our lover's face to his abdomen, Warren shivered inside me.

I can almost hear the strangled groan Dagan made right before he said, "I need to fuck right now. Get out of the way, Warren. Or I'm going to take your virgin ass!"

Warren didn't move.

Above me, Warren gasps and his eyes glaze over. Just as they had that night. Behind him, the flickering candlelight casts a shadowy outline of Dagan mounting our lover. Warren bucks on top of me, grinding his shaft into my greedy pussy then retreating as he impales himself on the ghost of Dagan's cock.

The carnal illusion floods my soul with passion. Wave after wave of pleasure crash over me, threatening to drown me in sensation. My orgasm triggers Warren's. Jets of his hot cum fill me as his cock pulses somewhere far below the surface of my belly. My muscles clamp around his jerking flesh, wringing every last drop of ecstasy from our climaxes.

I can't breathe. I can't move. I can't think or fear. All I can do is accept what he gives me and wish Dagan were here to share it.

A shockwave of ecstasy, magic and love radiates out from the juncture of our bodies. Warren tips his head back and roars with completion. A starburst of white light flares so bright I squint into the gleam for any sign of success even as I expect to burst into flames from the searing desire blazing inside me. Then the sparkle fades, leaving me gasping in the wake of our magically enhanced coupling.

Warren flops beside me when the black satin sheet across the room flutters to the ground. Nothing lies beneath it. For long moments, the only sounds in the room are the sputter of candles about to burn out, our harsh panting and the clank of the room's automatic shutters blocking out the breaking dawn.

I close my eyes, terrified. Have we failed? I prepare myself to surrender to the void in payment for the faulty spell. The death of a vampire leads to no afterlife.

CHAPTER FIVE

Instead of the abyss devoid of sound and light I expect, I hear the most beautiful thing in the entire universe.

Dagan's gruff, arousal-laden voice barks, "First, you disobey your king by dabbling in dark magic you don't fully understand. Now you two will stand aside and let your mate suffer?"

My eyelids fly open. Dagan kneels behind Warren, his gorgeous cock in hand. The sheen in his eyes proves he comprehends the gravity of the situation despite his flip comment. He guides his shaft along the furrow of Warren's ass but both of us are too exhausted, and overcome with relief, to do more than cling to each other as tears of gratitude roll over our cheeks.

"Dagan..." I try to express the hundreds of emotions swirling in my mind but it's unnecessary. All three of us understand what must happen. We require no instructions, the magic lives in us. Instincts drive Dagan to complete the ceremony by grounding himself in our world once more.

He jerks his shaft with lazy grace while he murmurs to us. "It was so dark, so cold. Then I saw a beam of light composed of brilliant colors. I knew it was you. Both of you. It was painfully beautiful, the way I feel when you're with me, when we're making love. It hurt to move, to swim against the current sweeping me away. But I couldn't let it take me. We belong together."

His last word draws out to a growl. He'd fought to return to us like the warrior king we've loved for eons. I've never craved him more. The tempo of his hand crescendos and his voice takes on an ancient inflection when he pronounces. "You are mine. And I am yours. Forever."

It's impossible to forget the moment he made that vow to me when we were new, barely turned vampires. There isn't a shred of doubt in my soul that reforming our sacred oath, including Warren in our sphere of mated bliss, is part of our destiny.

I surround Warren's trembling fingers with my own. Dagan uses his enhanced magic to move the three of us, still linked, to our marriage bed. Though I can recognize the fingerprint of his life force with my eyes closed, it is even more spectacular than before. Unbreakable.

The net of his unique power cradles us until we float onto the down mattress. I've always thought the enormous bed, raised on a gold-leafed dais, to be an over-extravagant indulgence by my romantic husband. At the dawn of this new phase of our lives, the ornate canopied enclosure makes the perfect backdrop for our extended pledges.

This time, sorcery ensures their truth. The Phoenix Incantation has granted all my seemingly futile hopes, my desperate wishes. No amount of time with the two men I love could suffice. I'll need eternity to illustrate the depth of my devotion. And bask in theirs in return.

In unrehearsed unison, Warren and I each claim one of Dagan's giant hands then recite the vow in return. "You are mine. And I am yours. Forever."

Dagan crushes me to his chest as he settles onto his side in the mountain of assorted pillows. He drags Warren closer until I am sandwiched between them. The heat of their toned muscles surrounds me but only provides a millionth of the warmth I derive from the emotions churning within my heart.

Above my head, Dagan whispers as he stares into our new mate's eyes. "Thank you both for the risk you took. It makes me ill enough to die all over again imagining what could have happened to you."

His burly arm drapes over Warren's waist, skimming my hip.

"We were coming for you, Warren. That day. Please believe

we wanted you long before this enchantment bound you to us."

The gentle caress of elegant fingers moves along my ribs then up Dagan's wrist. I turn until my back is snug against Dagan's chest so I can glimpse the peace in Warren's expression. He smiles at me then says, "I know."

He dips his head, nuzzling his nose against mine before nibbling at my lips. I sigh when he releases me. Then I tilt my face up to watch as he and Dagan exchange a fierce kiss. Dagan's hand slides up the flexed muscles of Warren's shoulder to anchor him in place. The corresponding throb of his rejuvenated erection on my stomach has me squirming.

"Take her. She is yours as well as mine." Dagan rasps in fragments between rough duels of their tongues.

Warren angles his hips then uses his power to align his cock with my welcoming flesh. He glides into me, filling me with one long stroke. The pleasure drives me past rational thought. I throw one leg over his hip to cling to him, though it would be impossible to get any closer. My lips latch onto the pulse in his throat but I force myself to refrain from the delicacy until the perfect moment.

They must hurry, I need to taste him. To seal our bond.

Lost in the rapture of his smooth thrusts, I hadn't noticed Dagan probing my rear with a tendril of his magic. The tiny stream embedded in me begins to expand, catching my attention, enhancing my pleasure. I moan when the air between my legs is formed into many tiny fingers that tease my sensitized pussy.

The flurry of motion draws the arousal dripping around Warren's cock to my ass. My lover fucks harder as several of the tendrils extend their reach, shimmering over his tight balls. I laugh at his tortured curse. My amusement is cut short when they continue growing until they undulate over my clit.

I clamp around Warren's cock and around the magic that has begun to spread my ass open in such gradual increments I feel only the pleasure and none of the pain. The excess moisture from my pussy is drawn onto the clenching ring of my ass, painted there with swirls of insubstantial contact that leave me craving more.

"Dagan, I need you." My fingernails rake Warren's back as I struggle to steal more of him, of them both, but I am pinned helpless between them.

"Shh, love. You'll have me. You always have me. Let me work you open, I don't want you to hurt for even a moment. No more suffering today." The mass of solidified air filling my rear bulges again, though nowhere near the girth of his mammoth cock. I don't care if it stings, I want him inside me. He'll ease the ache soon enough.

As though he senses my impatience, Warren redoubles his efforts to distract me. At the same time he lunges within my pussy, pummeling my sopping flesh, Dagan increases the swirls of his magic massaging my clit.

I cannot resist them. My spine arches, pressing my head into Dagan's shoulder. He devours my lips as he continues to prepare me. I fight the assault of ecstasy but I cannot hold on.

"Come for me, Amy." Warren groans as he observes the rapture that must be written on my face. His slick chest glides over mine, stroking the aching peaks of my breasts.

He grinds against me, driving me beyond control. I shatter around him, screaming his name even as Dagan expands the probe in my ass. Before the spasms of climax fade, Dagan replaces the shaft of air with his cock. I've never felt it this hard before. Huge, even for him, I see why he has insisted on waiting.

Dripping wet and ready, I expect him to impale me with ease. Yet he triggers an answering aftershock of desire with every thrust that works him a little deeper. When the head of his cock nudges Warren's stiff flesh through the thin tissue separating then, both of my mates groan.

My orgasm is endless, bursting in surge after surge as they refuse to let me relax. Dagan roars when he is finally seated to the root. His magic lifts us. We float over the bed—spinning, hovering so that both of my lovers can move freely within me. The vigorous lunges of their hungry bodies leave me incapacitated. All I can do is enjoy the gift of their passion.

My hair drapes around us like a curtain, or hangs beneath us like a waterfall as we spin and rock together. The remnants of my orgasm coalesce, building again into something more substantial.

"Yes, love. That's right. Take us with you this time." Dagan redoubles his efforts. Or maybe his control has disintegrated. He fucks me like a wild animal, though his hands are still tender when they caress the sides of my breasts. "I need to taste you."

The last is a ragged growl from his throat. The same urge burns my belly. Just the thought shoves me closer to the precipice. Warren moans then tilts his face to lick a path up Dagan's neck. My fangs rest over the artery exposed to me. When the pumping blood beneath Warren's skin bumps against my teeth, I am lost.

I come again, squeezing the shafts that fuck me together. The flexing of all my muscles sinks my teeth into Warren's neck. The delicious tang of his blood fills my mouth, gliding over my tongue. The erotic pain obliterates his control. He snarls as he erupts deep inside my pussy, still fucking as he bites Dagan. His essence is tinged with Dagan's flavor, the combination pure perfection to my taste buds.

Dagan surrenders, groaning as he pumps his seed into my ass. The razor sharp canines that pierce my artery trigger the last burst of my orgasm. Nothing can surpass the pleasure of feeding my mates. Dagan releases in a final fury of passion. His power sputters as his concentration evaporates. We tumble to the bed together.

The punctures on our necks heal instantly as our fangs are withdrawn. Warren lifts his head from its cushion on my breast, to lap tiny spatter marks from my cheek as *our* mate collapses beside us.

The moment the three of our essences have mingled, irrevocably blended, the taint of the poison lifts from my blood. A tingling sensation builds over my heart in an intricate design. Simultaneously, each of us glances down to discover our own matching brand.

A single phoenix, encased in a heart-shaped flame, rises above three separate figures—identical, everlasting and flawless.

Just as our love for each other will eternally be.

THANKS FOR READING!

Did you enjoy this book? If so, please leave a review and tell your friends. Word of mouth and online reviews are immensely helpful to authors and greatly appreciated.

To keep up with all the latest news about Jayne's books, appearances, merchandise, release info, exclusive excerpts and more, sign up for her newsletter at

www.jaynerylon.com/newsletter

More than 25 prizes are given out to subscribers in each monthly edition.

COOL GEAR FOR BIBLIOPHILES!

If you love Jayne's books, or reading in general, check out her shop for unique gear. You can get any of her print books personalized and autographed. In addition, there are t-shirts and hoodies with fun slogans about reading, tote bags for carrying all your books or eReaders, office supplies and more. Best of all you can buy ebooks directly from her site.

www.JayneRylon.com/shop

SNEAK PEEK – *RED LIGHT BOXSET*

Enjoy Jayne's style? Check out this edgy story of a sex worker in Amsterdam who falls in love with a client but doesn't plan to quit her job.
Try the first book (*Through My Window*) FREE!
Entire series only $4.99

I'm Star, a sex worker in Amsterdam's Red Light district. I invite you to step through my window. Careful, though. Observing my passionate exchanges may destroy your preconceptions.

I adore my profession. I'm many things in the course of one evening—whore, lover, nurse, psychologist and friend. But above all, I'm still a woman. Maybe the truths I've discovered about myself by serving others will help me deal with one customer who's come to mean more than all the others.

There's no doubt Rick desires me, but lately our business arrangement seems personal. How can I choose between the profession I love most, and the person I can't live without?
I'm greedy. I want both.

Step behind the glass and indulge your every urge in Amsterdam's flesh-filled pleasure district.

Through My Window
Red Light Series, Book One

"Through my window, a sea of strangers swirl and retreat like waves in an ocean of humanity. I brush my hair, fix my makeup and flip on the glaring red light in my booth before turning to face my audience on the other side of the glass."

For Star, this is another night on the job, though no two are ever alike. Adaptable and perceptive, she becomes many things in the course of one evening—whore, lover, nurse, psychologist and friend. But above all, she's still a woman. Join her, through her window.

Star
Red Light Series, Book Two

Star has seen it all as a sex worker in Amsterdam. She harnesses her intense sexuality to bring her clients satisfaction—or whatever else they desire. When one of her favorites, Rick, makes an unusual proposition, she accepts the rare opportunity.

She finds herself onstage, the lead in a naughty Christmas pageant, indulging in electrophilia where anyone can witness her client-turned-costar give her a present she'll never forget. The sparks between them grow into something more, forcing them to decide if they're strong enough to seek more than simple pleasure together.

Can't Buy Love
Red Light Series, Book Three

What man would be crazy enough to date a whore? Star is a sex worker in Amsterdam's red light district. After an intimate exchange between her and Rick, she's hoped to take their adventure into affection farther. Too bad he's disappeared for weeks.

When he resurfaces to deliver her portion of the paycheck they'd earned by starring in a live sex show together, the magnetism between them proves irresistible. In the wake of undeniable passion, they're left wondering if they can make a relationship work in unconventional circumstances.

They're both convinced you can buy sex, but you can't buy love. And nothing else will satisfy their hunger for each other.

Free for All
Red Light Series, Book Four

After a courtship filled with nights steamy enough to thaw the lingering winter chill, Sarah is finally beginning to believe she might have found the one man who can support her career as a sex worker in Amsterdam's Red Light district. But when she asks around, it's clear Rick isn't taking advantage of the freedom their open relationship offers. None of the sexiest girls in the district have serviced him for months.

Afraid of losing the star of her extra-naughty dreams, Sarah confronts her boyfriend about his change of heart. Rick confesses he's no longer interested in wild times without her. Instead, he'd like to try experimenting with multiple partners, show off his sexy woman and revel in the company of like-minded hedonists. Fortunately, he knows just the place for a debauched experience wicked enough to make even an experienced hooker blush.

A sexual free-for-all is on the menu at one of Amsterdam's infamous swingers' clubs, and by the end of the night, Sarah is going to get the surprise of her life.

ABOUT THE AUTHOR

Jayne Rylon is a *New York Times* and *USA Today* bestselling author. She received the 2011 Romantic Times Reviewers' Choice Award for Best Indie Erotic Romance. Her stories used to begin as daydreams in seemingly endless business meetings, but now she is a full time author, who employs the skills she learned from her straight-laced corporate existence in the business of writing. She lives in Ohio with two cats and her husband, the infamous Mr. Rylon. When she can escape her purple office, she loves to travel the world, avoid speeding tickets in her beloved Sky, and–of course–read.

Jayne loves to chat with fans.
You can find her at the following places when she's procrastinating:

Twitter: @JayneRylon
Facebook: http://www.facebook.com/jayne.rylon
Website: www.jaynerylon.com
Newsletter: www.jaynerylon.com/newsletter
Email: contact@jaynerylon.com

OTHER BOOKS BY JAYNE RYLON

Available Now

COMPASS BROTHERS
Northern Exposure
Southern Comfort
Eastern Ambitions
Western Ties

COMPASS GIRLS
Winter's Thaw
Hope Springs
Summer Fling

HOT RODS
King Cobra
Mustang Sally
Super Nova
Rebel On The Run

MEN IN BLUE
Night is Darkest
Razor's Edge
Mistress's Master
Spread Your Wings

PICK YOUR PLEASURES
Pick Your Pleasure
Pick Your Pleasure 2

PLAY DOCTOR
Dream Machine
Healing Touch

POWERTOOLS
Kate's Crew
Morgan's Surprise
Kayla's Gift
Devon's Pair
Nailed To The Wall
Hammer It Home

RACING FOR LOVE
Driven
Shifting Gears

RED LIGHT (STAR)
Through My Window
Star
Can't Buy Love
Free For All

SINGLE TITLES
Nice and Naughty
Picture Perfect
Phoenix Incantation
Where There's Smoke

AUDIOBOOKS
Nice and Naughty
Dream Machine
Night is Darkest
Report For Booty
Powertools
Kate's Crew
Morgan's Surprise
Kayla's Gift
Devon's Pair

Coming Soon

COMPASS GIRLS
Falling Softly

HOT RODS
Swinger Style
Barracuda's Heart
Touch of Amber
Long Time Coming

MEN IN BLUE
Spread Your Wings
Wounded Hearts
Bound For You

PICK YOUR PLEASURES
Pick Your Pleasure 3

PLAY DOCTOR
Developing Desire

SINGLE TITLE
Four-ever Theirs

JAYNE RECOMMENDS...

Burn With Me
By R.G. Alexander
For more information visit www.RGAlexander.com

She walks a tightrope between light and dark. Danger and passion. Obsession and love...

Fireborne, Book 1

Aziza Jane Stewart is living on borrowed time, and making a few mistakes in London seems like a good way to go out with a bang. But when two compelling strangers draw her into an ancient conflict, she realizes her curse isn't about death at all...it's about the power within her.

The sexy giant following her says he can smell trouble on her skin, the smokeless fire and magic of the demons he was born and bred to hunt. Brandon may be an enforcer, but his reaction to her is anything but adversarial. Ram, her new Jinn shadow, will do whatever it takes to come between them, and he's just as hard for Aziza to resist.

When her dark family legacy burns to the surface, whom can Aziza trust? The alpha male who pushes all her hot buttons, the Jinn who seduces her in dreams, or the emerging Fireborne within? As danger circles closer, she must learn to embrace her newfound powers—and trust someone with her heart—before she becomes the final casualty.

Warning: Explicit content, magic, danger, voyeurism, chains, a secret ménage and carnal deeds of devilish debauchery at every other turn. Basically...fasten your seatbelts and get ready to burn.

Made in the USA
Columbia, SC
24 May 2019